W9-BQW-156

CRITICS CHEER FOR KIMBERLY RAYE!

"Ms. Raye has written an enthralling paranormal . . . capturing the reader's attention and never letting go. 4 1/2 stars!"

—*Romantic Times* on *A Stranger's Kiss*

"*Midnight Fantasies* is . . . a very funny book, and a hot one, too."

—*All About Romance*

"A rip-rollicking, hilarious adventure that will steal your heart and have you laughing out loud. Ms. Raye has penned a delightfully different time-travel."

—*Romantic Times* on *Midnight Fantasies*

"Kimberly Raye has a unique and special talent that will no doubt be heard and remembered for years to come!"

—*Affaire de Coeur*

"If you're lamenting the lack of sexy, funny, character-driven romances on the bookshelves these days, you absolutely will not want to miss reading . . . *Midnight Kisses*."

—*All About Romance*

"Ms. Raye's creative plotting and vivid characterization herald a strong new voice in romantic fiction."

—*Romantic Times*

A MIRACLE?

Sophie told Beth goodbye, punched the END button on her cell phone, and then turned back to the mirror. Letting out a deep, exasperated breath, she shoved a piece of stray hair that had come loose from her ponytail behind her ear, wiped at her watery eyes, and turned to leave the bathroom.

"Stop praying for miracles," she murmured as she pushed through the door.

The sun had already started to set, and shadows crowded the empty hallway. The only light came from a neon EXIT sign at the far end just to the right of the elevator.

"You're on your own tonight," she said to herself. The way she had been her entire childhood and most of her adolescence.

Alone.

Lonely.

"Not tonight, Sophie." She heard the voice a heartbeat before she felt a hard, muscular body step up behind her. "Tonight, it's you and me."

KIMBERLY RAYE

A STRANGER'S DESIRE

LOVE SPELL NEW YORK CITY

LOVE SPELL®

January 2003

Published by

Dorchester Publishing Co., Inc.
276 Fifth Avenue
New York, NY 10001

ISBN: 0-505-52504-6

A STRANGER'S DESIRE

Chapter One

He existed solely for a woman's pleasure.

He was the erotic whisper in the dead of night. The seductive touch in a sexy dream. The tall, dark, tempting stranger who melted a female's resolve with one smoldering glance.

His touch was sometimes slow and sure, at other times fierce and primal.

His kiss could be deep and wet, or soft and chaste.

His words ranged from sweet and cajoling to raw and commanding.

His scent mesmerized with the deep, earthy aroma of leather and sawdust, or teased with the ripe scent of tropical fruit baking under a hot Caribbean sun.

He could be either blonde or brunette. Tall or

short. Scruffy or clean-shaven. Heavily muscled or lanky and slim.

He was sometimes a poet, sometimes a rock star. A football player or a brain surgeon.

Outgoing or shy.

An intellectual or a working man.

Whatever the fantasy, whatever the deepest, most erotic desire, he knew and he played that role.

Such was his purpose. His duty. His destiny.

All to please a woman.

To satisfy her in ways no man ever could, for he was more than a man.

He was the embodiment of sex. A spirit fueled by the ancient fire of lust. A carnal being insatiable in his need, desperate for a woman's touch, her smell, her feel.

A sexual demon.

Cain was an incubus, and this woman *wanted him.*

He saw it in the way her eyelids lowered and her eyes darkened as she met his gaze across the immaculate kitchen. She spent the majority of her time here—when she wasn't transporting her kids to and from soccer games, leading the local PTA bake sales, organizing fund-raising functions for various charities, or playing the dutiful wife to a husband who'd long since forgotten about her.

Her needs.

Her desires.

2

Those were all lost in the past.

But Cain knew what she yearned for, what she lay awake at night thinking about, hoping for, wanting with all her heart and soul.

Him.

He smelled that truth as she stepped toward him, closer, closer; the sweet, musty scent of wet, warm, desperate female filled his nostrils and sent a burst of heat to his already throbbing erection.

Yes, me.

He leaned down and his mouth found the soft skin of her neck. She was sweet, her skin slightly salty, flavored by a hint of the raspberry-scented lotion she'd slathered on just moments before his arrival. In anticipation of it.

For *she* had initiated this deal.

She'd dreamt of him night after night. She'd cried out for him in her sleep, begged for him in the bright light of day, and now he was here.

She moaned, and he leaned back to stare down at her. Her lips parted, inviting him to kiss her, begging him to take her away, to give her the sweet, consuming heat that she had once known with others, that had become only a vague memory; to prove to her that she wasn't as unattractive as she felt, as worn out, as used up, as old.

Hardly.

She was beautiful, with her warm chocolate

3

eyes and her full lips. Her hips were well-rounded thanks to two children, but that simply made her all the more womanly.

Voluptuous.

Desirable.

And that was how he saw all women—regardless of size and shape, blonde or brunette, short or tall. Cain the Slayer desired all females.

And they desired him.

"Kiss me," she breathed.

He leaned down, but he didn't do as she asked. Evasiveness was his tool. He used it to prolong the seduction, the anticipation, to make the inevitable coupling all the sweeter.

He swept his tongue down the curve of her neck until he felt the frantic pulse beating just below the surface. He licked and nibbled and tasted the salty sweetness of her skin, the desperation, the need.

He felt her lust too in the eager way she clung to him, in her fingers clutching at his shirt, in her breasts that pressed against him, the nipples like two pinpoints of fire drilling into his skin.

Yet, even without these evidences of her desire for him, he would simply *know*. Such knowledge, when it came, rang deep inside Cain. It was a certainty that had nothing to do with those five senses so vital to mortals, and everything to do with an inborn sixth sense—a sense that had made him extraordinary even when he'd lived and breathed as a mortal over one thousand years ago. A gift he'd tried hard to hide as a child. He'd been fearful of being singled out like his mother, of being persecuted and murdered.

He'd witnessed her death on that cold, dark night as he lay pretending to be asleep while she urged him with her mind not to look.

"Do not open your eyes, my sweet son. Just listen to my voice and know that I love you. They are coming, but stay where you are. Hidden. Stay asleep. Stay safe. Now and always."

Like any curious child, he'd looked, but not until her voice had faded. He'd looked, and he'd seen the chaos erupt as strangers burst into his family's small dwelling on the coast of Finland. Strangers who proceeded to do their worst while he crouched, terrified, in the hay of his bed.

He'd climbed out and looked at his mother afterward. The blood running from her mouth and nose, the empty look of death in her glazed eyes: it was a sight that haunted him from then on. But as he grew, it helped him. Where he'd been fearful before, the memories of his mother's death embittered him. They hardened him. They made him bold, reckless, and determined to use all the gifts with which he'd been born.

He'd become a slayer.

He'd led campaign after campaign, determined to push out the invaders, any who sought to threaten his homeland. He'd done so without a care. He'd flirted with death, daring it to knock on his door and claim him the way it had claimed his mother that night, and later, the way it claimed his warrior father.

He'd used all his power to help his people, to lead them victorious through battles that would have seen them slaughtered were it not for his leadership. And his gift, his sixth sense, had shown him how. He'd seen all obstacles before they presented themselves; he'd glimpsed his struggles' outcomes by joining hands with those who would fight with him. He would see their future, their defeats and their triumphs, and he was able to use that knowledge to choose wisely his course of action.

At the same time as his battle victories gained him property and notoriety, they also created enemies. There were many who wanted to see him dead, many who tried on more than one occasion to kill him. And they'd nearly succeeded one early morning while he lay asleep. Were it not for a sweet, young Viking maiden who'd seen the attack and come to his aid—cleansed and bound his wounds—he would have bled to death.

She'd saved him, then—not only from death but from himself. She'd given him a reason to care, to exercise caution, to simply enjoy being a man with a man's needs and desires. He'd turned away from his gift and tucked it away, eager to forget the past and leave it behind. Eager to leave behind the darkness.

As if such a thing were possible. One could never escape oneself.

His ability, like the darkness that surrounded him, had remained, followed him beyond, into this eternity of undeath and enslavement that he now lived out. It remained with him, still potent, as he continued his blind service to the carnal fire that had been lit deep inside of him.

His lust.

His punishment.

His penance.

Shaking off his reverie, as he always did after thinking too long on the past, he focused on the woman in his arms and let the rest slip away. He would fulfill his duty now. He would touch her, though he wouldn't join hands. He wouldn't look into her future and see the results of the choice she was about to make. Her future wasn't his concern. He cared only for his own present.

There was only now.

Only this.

Always this. . . .

"Please." The breathless plea whispered past her lips as he rotated his pelvis against the sensitive space between her thighs. *"Please."*

It wasn't enough.

He needed to hear the words.

7

He *had* to hear them, otherwise he couldn't give her the pleasure she so desperately craved. No matter how much she wanted him. No matter how much he wanted her. No matter that the proof vibrated through him, electrified every nerve until he felt ready to explode.

Not yet.

Not without her consent.

He started to demand as much, her consent, but deep inside he felt a moment's hesitation. The urge to push her away and save her from herself bubbled up in him and he stiffened.

No!

The command echoed through him and his every muscle went rigid. He couldn't do this. He shouldn't do it, for he knew what awaited this woman should she give in to temptation. As soon as she surrendered, she would become just another soul doomed to the Darkness after death. Her future would be sealed. *Damnation.*

"Do what you will, but I want her. I will have her."

The deep voice in his brain stirred his memory, reminded Cain that if he didn't take this woman, do as she asked, another would. The Dark One hungered for souls far too much to let even one slip by.

Particularly a soul this ripe, this ready.

There were many more of Cain's kind who would feel no hesitation, no remorse or regret, nothing save the lust driving them to touch and

8

stroke and *feel*, for such was their punishment. Their eternal duty.

It was his duty now, too.

Now and for always.

The woman's hands slid down Cain's chest, to his throbbing sex. Fire swept through him, setting every nerve ablaze. Need overwhelmed his conscience like a huge gust of wind kills a single, flickering flame. Though he'd wanted to stop, he knew now that he couldn't.

Unless she stopped him.

She held the power. This woman was the one who would choose what happened next, for she was the one who must make the final decision. She'd already requested his presence, determined to feel something besides loneliness, however briefly, and regardless of the cost. But although it was not too late for her to save herself, either way it was time for truth between them.

"What do you want, love?" he asked.

"This," the woman breathed. She rubbed her body against him as her gaze met his. "You. Take me."

And the choice was made.

Chapter Two

Sophie Alexander was about to make a deal with the Devil.

"That's Prince of Darkness, my dear. Or there's the ever-popular Lucifer. Or Satan. There's also the more aesthetically pleasing Lord of the Night. King of Demons. Hades' Top Dog. Commander-in-Chief of the Inferno-Down-Under. Take your pick." The vision arched one perfectly shaped blond brow and shrugged. "I don't mean to carry on so, but 'Devil' is just so cliché—don't you think?"

"I . . ." Sophie couldn't form a coherent sentence.

Forget thinking.

The only thing she could manage to do was breathe as she stared up at the devastatingly handsome man standing smack dab in the middle of her living room.

He wore a sinister-looking long, black robe, but that's where the expected ended. He had no horns or fangs. No scaly skin or forked tail. Rather, this conjuration looked like a sun-kissed Brad Pitt from *Legends of the Fall*, his hair long, his eyes as gray as smoke. As translucent.

They were reflective, too. As her gaze met his, Sophie could see herself in their shimmering depths. Her hair was pulled back in a tight ponytail, so she saw only her face. Her eyes were large and round, red-rimmed; her cheeks still shimmered with tears.

I'm crying.

She'd become so accustomed to it over the past year and a half that she hadn't even noticed. Frantically she wiped at her cheeks, but it did nothing to hide the sorrow in her eyes.

The desperation.

The excitement.

Her heart pounded and her blood rushed and her hands trembled.

The incantation worked!

"Of course it worked," her conjuration told her, his silvery gaze shifting to the large white candle that sat in the center of her coffee table. Its flame flickered and the smell of sugar cookies wafted through the room. "Although, I must admit I would have preferred black candles, or

11

maybe a red one. Something to actually set the mood for my visit. It seems more like you were expecting a visit from your grandma."

"It's all I had. That and those small votives from the Candle Factory over on Fifth. They're vanilla."

The man made a face. "And to think I came all the way from the Other Side for this. Don't they have any good shops selling my stuff in Chicago? Or maybe a voodoo hut? Voodoo's not a religion I endorse, mind you, but it's definitely closer to my taste than any of the others. I'm sure their shops would have *dozens* of black candles." He paused for a moment, looking thoughtful. "Now, who was that famous voodoo priestess that gained so much notoriety? Marie something or other. Now *there* was a woman who knew how to really summon a spirit. She not only lit things up with candles; she used actual bonfires. And a big black cauldron. And lots of dead chickens." He let loose a low whistle. "Now *that* was a woman out to make an impression."

"I do have a purple candle over in the corner," Sophie managed to say after several swallows. "That's close to black." It was a crazy comment, but then the entire situation bordered on lunacy.

"Purple is better, but still a tad . . . Christian." He sighed and clicked his tongue.

The *Devil*.

The Devil.

"Not as Christian, however, as using that repulsive D word."

"You can read my thoughts," Sophie blurted, still trying to comprehend what was happening. She'd cast a spell and summoned the Devil, who was now here reading her thoughts.

"I can do many things, sweet Sophie, which is why you called me." His gaze glittered like stars in a midnight sky. "So, tell me what you want."

"I . . ." She licked her lips, ready to burst with the desperation burning inside her. Yet a small part—that part of her that kept insisting she forfeit one too many hours of sleep in favor of working on her latest product for the cosmetics company where she headed research and development, a product that would not only keep her company in the number-one spot, but save her goddaughter's life, as well—that part of her couldn't accept the possible solution this conjuration presented. The situation was simply too unbelievable.

An hour ago, she'd been tucking the girl into bed. A half hour ago, she'd been popping open a bottle of champagne, determined to celebrate the good news—that her sweet, precious Kara had no new signs of cancer. Fifteen minutes ago, she'd been forcing down each sip, all the while trying to tell herself that this happy state would last. Ten minutes ago, she'd given up lec-

13

turing herself in favor of doing something to see that the cancer stayed away. Something crazy. Something impossible.

Now she was talking to the devil himself.

Her brain rushed back and relived the moments leading up to this surreal one. She saw again her goddaughter curl up under the blankets, the girl's eyes shadowed with dark circles, her cheeks pale where they should have glowed with youth and optimism. The memory knifed right through Sophie and stirred her anger anew.

She'd tried everything: new doctors, experimental drugs, herbal remedies, prayer.

Nothing had worked.

She'd been out of hope, out of answers. She'd been flipping between stations on the TV, alternating between the Sci-Fi Channel and Country Music Television. She'd settled on the former and an old movie about a man who'd sold his soul to the Devil in exchange for a lottery ticket.

Ridiculous. Yet, with each sip of champagne and each tear that slid down her cheek, she'd started to actually wonder.

What if?

And so, in a half-drunken, wishful stupor, laughing at herself and the absurdity of her actions, she'd lit every candle she could find, turned off the lights and recited the spell the actor had used in the movie.

She hadn't really believed, had she? No. This

had been grasping at straws, a last-ditch effort to avoid accepting her fear that Kara's cancer was only on temporary hold, that the girl was still dying but no one knew.

That it was still just a matter of time.

Unless . . .

Sophie blinked, her eyes bleary from lack of sleep. But the image before her didn't disappear. He simply smiled, his mirror-like eyes filled with a knowing light.

He read her disbelief.

He read every thought racing through her head.

He was the Devil. *The* Devil.

"There you go again." He shook his head, his mouth crooking into a grin. "But I shan't waste my time scolding you. We have more important matters with which to contend." He rubbed his hands together before extending his arms skyward, then braced as if he'd set himself up as a lightning rod. "Go ahead and do it."

"Do what?"

"Touch me. You mortals believe what you can see and touch. You can obviously see me, so all that's left is to reach out and . . ."

He continued to smile, but the expression had left his eyes. His gaze fixed on hers, those silver depths shimmering, mirroring all: her pale face streaked with those damnable tears, her lips still wet from choking down tasteless champagne.

15

Frustration rose up inside Sophie, gobbling up her shock and hesitation and the smidgeon of fear that curled her stomach. She drew in a deep breath, extended her hand toward him and . . .

Heat.

A sudden scorching heat overwhelmed her; she felt zapped as if by a bolt of electricity that sucked the air from her lungs. Snatching her hand back, she stared down at her fingertips, expecting to see singed skin.

Nothing. Not a black mark or a wisp of smoke. Just smooth, pale flesh that hummed from the contact.

"I know, I know. It's not quite like touching a human being. Certainly not like the time you held hands with that boy back in the sixth grade behind the Piggly Wiggly."

Sophie's head snapped up and her gaze met the Devil's.

"Ah, so you remember that." He arched a brow. "He was the one who kissed you and later blabbed to the entire gym class. The news spread to their parents and then to your parents." He shook his head. "My, but they didn't like that one bit. Their precious genius, their little girl mingling with the commons."

"They wanted better for me. They loved me."

"That's what they said, but you didn't believe it, did you, Sophie? You knew that was just an excuse. They wanted to mold you to fit what

16

they wanted you to be. Bigger than everyone else. Better than everyone else. Smarter than everyone else. But you weren't about to fall for it. That kiss was a sweet taste of rebellion, and you wanted more. Remember that time you got up-close-and-personal in the back seat of that old beat-up Chevy pick-up? My, but that was your rebellion at its finest."

"How do you . . ." The question faded, as did the last remnant of her doubt in this conjuration's identity.

"That was the first time you went parking," he went on. "He was a hockey player, wasn't he? A senior, while you were a lowly freshman. He was so strong and warm, and he smelled like that cheap aftershave they sold down at the corner drugstore."

"Texas Rain."

He shook his head. "Atrocious stuff, if you ask me."

But she'd loved it and she'd loved him, and her parents had hated both.

"I could spritz on some Texas Rain for you, Sophie, but it wouldn't make me smell any more mortal. You see, I'm not flesh and blood." He winked. "But I can be just as fleshly. Just as erotic."

In the blink of an eye, Sophie found herself staring at an empty living room. Her breath caught and she started to turn, only to find herself paralyzed by heat behind her, surrounding her, seeping into her body and quickening her blood.

A heartbeat later, the Devil's voice slid into her ears, charging her nerve endings, making her entire body buzz as much as the slight hint of contact had a moment before.

"I can stir you more than that sweet-smelling hockey player, Sophie—if given the chance and your consent." His heat, like an invisible hand, skimmed the back of her neck, sweeping down her arm and up again. "Just say the word, and I can make you feel the very same thing you felt back then."

His voice grew lower, deeper. "Is that what you want from me, sweet Sophie?"

The question hung in the air surrounding her as the razor-sharp point of the Devil's nail touched her shoulder and traced a path along it. She felt a sticky trickle of wetness and glanced down to see the bright red drip of blood on the floor. Yet there was no pain. She felt only the slow movement of his nail, the pattern mesmerizing as it was traced over and over.

"Don't you want to feel warm again? Isn't that why you called? Because you're lonely? Because you hole up here in this apartment and spend all of your time taking care of your poor Kara when you should be out having fun like every other single female your age? Aren't you desperate to live again, where you've merely been existing these past few years since you were burdened with a sick child?"

He was so close and so warm, yet at the same time a chill worked its way down Sophie's spine and back up again, like a snake slithering and twining through her innards. His words echoed in her ears. *Burdened. Sick child.*

She stiffened.

"Don't you already know what I want? If you're really and truly as powerful as it's said, you should know."

Immediately, he stood in front of her again. "Of course I do, but I need to hear the request from you. I have rules I must abide by, you know. One is that I can only respond to a verbal request. While I'm fully aware of everything going on in that pretty little head of yours, I can only help if you ask me."

She indicated the briefcase open on the floor next to the couch. A mess of notes spilled out onto the carpet next to her half-drunk bottle of champagne.

"Do you know what all that is?"

"Atrocious handwriting, sweet Sophie." He smiled. "Is that why you've made all this fuss? Because you need my expert penmanship?"

"Those notes are my future. My incomplete future." She shook her head. "I can't find it." Tears stung her eyes again. "I've been working on this nearly night and day for the past several months, but I'm still not there. I'm close. I just need one more ingredient. Just one."

"Which is?"

"I don't know. That's why you're here. I need the final ingredient. The one that will pull this formula completely together."

The Devil shrugged. "Perhaps this ingredient you seek does not exist. Maybe you've wasted an entire sugar-cookie candle for nothing," he suggested.

"It *does* exist. I've narrowed it down to a family of iron-oxide stabilizers, but I don't know which one is *the* one, or how much, or if I need a combination of a few rather than one specific oxide."

The Devil shook his head. "It sounds like you need to do more testing."

"I don't have time. I need it now. That's why I called you."

"You want me to give you the answer." He sounded mildly peeved.

"You're my last hope."

The Devil laughed. Where he'd sounded charming and seductive before, his tone now held a shade of malice. "I've been called many things, but rarely a last hope. You *do* know what you're asking, don't you?" He smiled. "My help commands a price. I don't distribute answers to people's questions merely to amuse myself."

"I know that. There's nothing free in this life, and obviously not in the one beyond."

He arched an eyebrow. "Smart. I like that."

His expression shifted, his gaze taking on a gleam as hard, as sharp as the razor-like steak knives that sat in Sophie's butcher block. "Tell me, sweet girl, what you will give your last hope in return for his help?"

The question echoed through her head as Sophie thought of the endless testing that still awaited her, of all the time-consuming, tedious experiments, one after the other, with no guarantee that the discovery would ever come. What if it did not come before Kara drew her last and final breath?

The fear was overwhelming, but then it receded. The answer echoed deep in Sophie's heart, for she knew what she had to do.

"The only thing I have of value to offer someone like you," she answered. "The only thing you want."

"And that is?"

Sophie drew in a deep breath, met the Devil's gaze and watched herself speak the words that would change her life forever. "My soul."

Chapter Three

"I knew there was a reason you were my favorite."

At the sound of the deep, familiar voice, Cain turned away from the computer screen. His gaze cut through the bedroom where only moments ago he'd bedded his latest assignment. Moonlight filtered through the large bay window, pushing back the darkness and illuminating the woman who slept soundly in the king-sized four-poster bed.

His attention shifted beyond, to the farthest corner. The darkness stirred and shifted, gaining size and shape. He watched as the Evil One materialized from the shadows, the portal between the mortal world and the Inferno.

Those shadows were the only way in, and the

only way out, before the sun rose and chased away the Prince of Darkness and all his minions. Including Cain. But there were still a few hours before dawn cracked open the sky, there was still time before he had to return to the Underworld, to rejuvenate for the next night's endeavors. He'd intended to while away some of the time on his conquest's computer.

"Always working." The Evil One moved nearer Cain and stared past him at the computer screen and the depicted sandy beach filled with scantily clad women. The sun blazed overhead, reflecting off the deep blue water of the Riviera. "Scoping out prospective victims. I like that."

Cain gave one last glance at the brilliant Southern European sun and punched several buttons. The computer screen flickered and darkened, and Cain turned his full attention to his master.

Today the Prince of Darkness looked more like the Earl of Ordinary with his tan shorts, white T-shirt and red baseball cap. He looked an everyday Joe. Inconspicuous. Harmless.

To Cain, that was. But to some unlucky soul, somewhere, this version of the Devil was his worst nightmare. This vision was what he feared when he turned off the lights and crawled between his covers. This was what he tossed and turned and worried over until morn-

23

ing finally arrived and chased the darkness away.

The Evil One had many faces, just as he had many names. Modern Judeo-Christian cultures called him the Devil. Back in Cain's day, among the Vikings, he'd been referred to as Loki, god of destruction, or Aud, the son of darkness. Throughout the years, he'd been called everything from Pan and Cernunnos to Lucifer. He'd taken on every form, from snakes to beetles to those rock stars who incited such anger in Christian Fundamentalists.

The Evil One was a chameleon, changing with the times, adapting to each situation, molding to fit each individual's weaknesses. Only one thing about him remained the same: his eyes. They were an irridescent silver. Translucent. Reflective. They mirrored a person's own image so that when one stared into them, he saw himself stripped bare of all pretense; he saw his own shortcomings, his insecurity, his anxiety, his fear.

Cain stared into his master's tell-tale gaze. The image that greeted him had short, dark hair and a clean-shaven jaw—far from the Viking who'd once stood up and challenged the renegade Hasting's plan to attack the city of Troyes back in 891.

He'd been strong then. Merciless. He'd followed Hasting because the man was intent on establishing a homeland. In the beginning that was why. But that had changed as greed set in.

He hadn't been greedy for booty, though. No, he'd had other reasons for joining the fight. He'd lived for every battle, relished the rush that came with combat. He'd fought under the pretense of something noble, but he'd really been fighting to slake his bloodlust, to conquer the memories of his past. That had become his reason for existence.

And Hasting. He'd challenged the man, but not for the right reasons, not because he'd seen the repercussions, the slaughter that would come. He'd done it merely for the challenge. The *fight*. Not because of the vision he'd had when he'd touched Hasting's hand. Not because he'd wanted to do good. Not because he'd wanted to avert the murders of the people of Troyes.

Yes, he'd challenged Hasting, but he hadn't been able to stop him. There had been too many other greedy men who followed the renegade, and without righteousness on his side Cain had been quickly overwhelmed.

It was the same now.

Of course, the greed that now attacked Cain was no longer a lust for blood. His need was for something else, invisible, overwhelming, merciless. It was a carnal desire that gripped him, held him captive and forced upon him its will. It was simply a need for sex. But it was no less unconquerable.

He stared at his reflection in the Evil One's eyes: a clean-cut, three-piece-suit type who'd been the ultimate fantasy man of this woman who lay sound asleep in her bed not three feet away. Her soft, contented snore echoed through the room. She was exhausted, spent, at peace.

For now.

If he hadn't known better, Cain would have sworn he saw guilt flicker in the fiery depths of his eyes. But the truth was, he could feel no guilt. He could feel no remorse. Not since he'd lived and breathed as a man.

Resigned, he watched his reflection change. His hair grew, falling past his shoulders; the color lightened to blond. The faint shadow of a beard appeared on his jaw. His eyes glowed a fierce red, burning up the earlier green before cooling to a deep, midnight blue. His complexion darkened to a sun-kissed copper, and his shoulders broadened. Soon he resembled his original self.

He sighed.

He looked and felt like flesh and blood right now, like the old self he had once been. During the night's darkest hours when the veil between the world's was at its thinnest, he could look like this. But looks were deceiving.

He wasn't himself but an immortal. He was a collection of energy that drew its power from the darkness. A shadow of the man he'd once

26

been. A demonic spirit doomed to seduction. An incubus.

"You do enjoy the Viking thing, don't you? What is it with all of my incubi? Always shunning the guises they take in favor of the image of their former self."

Cain shrugged. "It's what I'm used to."

"It's *boring*, dear boy. Variety is the spice of life."

"This isn't life. It's death."

"A mere technicality." The Evil One winked before glancing down at his own attire. "While I enjoy variety, I do have to admit that I'm not as taken with this particular get-up as I could be. Beige shorts are most certainly not my thing. But, alas, duty calls."

"Been out tormenting some poor baseball fan?"

"Poor? Quite the opposite. He's the president and CEO of a multi-million dollar company. He's also a father of four who never tossed around the ball with any of his boys. He doesn't know a bat from a pogo stick. His youngest entered them in a pitching competition and he's spent a lot of sleepless nights worried about failing miserably."

"And he'll spend another, no doubt, tonight."

"Not if he seeks my help. I'll guarantee success and give him instant rest."

"A *temporary* rest."

"Yes. Once he kicks the bucket, then the party

starts." The Prince of Sin frowned. "So long as Celeste keeps her nose out of my business." He shook his head as if exasperated. "That damned female is always sticking her nose where it doesn't belong."

"Celeste?"

"As if she can really stop me," he went on, oblivious to Cain's question. "With her pretty smile and those angelic eyes." He shook his head as if trying to clear his head of some unwanted image. "She thinks she can undo anything I do, but she's got another think coming." His eyes flared bright red. Heat flooded the room, enveloping Cain and pressing the air from his lungs.

"I am the one with true power." The Evil One's deep, guttural voice boomed through the room, echoed in Cain's ears for moments afterward.

As quickly as it came, the heat subsided. The air cooled back to its previous temperature, and Cain could breathe once again.

"Ah, thankfully mortals these days are eager for instant gratification. It makes what Celeste offers—eternal life and all that bunk—seem paltry in comparison." The Lord of the Night gave Cain a knowing look and indicated the computer screen. It flickered on, and the image of the Riviera returned. "Not that instant gratification is a longing only known by mortals. You, yourself, are quite fond of it."

"It's what I am."

The Dark One's gaze narrowed, glittered like chips of polished silver. "What I made you, dear Cain. Lest your forget."

"I don't want to forget." *If only*.

The Devil smiled. "And that's why you're my favorite. Ah . . ." He indicated a woman on the computer screen. "Now, here's a sweet one just ripe for picking."

The woman was topless, wore only a small thong to cover her femininity. She was beautiful, but there was a sadness apparent in her eyes, and that's what drew the Evil One's attention more than her curvaceous body. She was needy, desperate, and that enticed him.

It drew Cain as well, stirred the lust deep inside him. He knew how sweet a desperate woman tasted. How warm she felt. How wet.

A restlessness filled him, a hunger, as if it had been years since he'd had a woman rather than the mere minutes that had just passed. His sex throbbed in response. "Is she the next assignment?"

"So eager to move on?" The Dark One motioned to the sleeping woman on the bed. "You've barely finished with the Internet designer here. Besides, it's almost daylight."

Cain shook his head. "This is the housewife. I did the designer last night. And we've got a few good hours left."

"Ah, yes. Now I remember." The Devil waved

a hand. "Things have been so busy lately. So many souls on the verge of corruption."

Exactly the way Cain liked it. The more women who needed him, the more he touched, tasted, seduced, the less he thought about his mistakes, the less he worried about making peace with his past. Then, for a time, the images stopped creeping into his mind. The voices. The memories.

A vision struck him: a woman, tears on her face, a small child in her arms. Her mouth opened and closed, but Cain couldn't hear what she was saying. Lust beat at his senses; his curse was awake inside of him and ravenous.

It was time for the next assignment.

But who? Not this brunette. He'd been considering a different prey, a different woman. Or, more accurately, *women*.

"So what about these twins?" He punched a button on the computer and the screen flashed. The images of two brunettes appeared: familiar faces to any American who kept up with politics. These twins were the twenty-something daughters of right-wing conservative congressman Ben Jacey.

The congressman supported the death penalty, opposed abortion, and was a staunch advocate for censorship of libraries. He and his wife had been lobbying for strong censorship in the schools for years, and they'd raised their daughters to uphold their strong family values and strict political platform. But the twins weren't nearly as devout as their parents. They'd resisted temptation so far, through college somehow, but were both suffocating beneath their parents' strict rules.

They weren't much different from any of the other children of conservative parents—with one exception. They were high-profile. Their fall would be public and give the Evil One that much more pleasure. He thrived on power. Taking the souls of the daughters of one of America's most prominent right wingers would be a huge coup for him. A political victory, so to speak.

Cain wasn't nearly as concerned with who the twins were so much as the fact that there were two of them.

The Evil One smiled. "This is better than twins."

Cain arched an eyebrow. "Triplets."

"Better."

"Quadruplets?"

The Evil One shook his head. "This isn't just about numbers, dear boy." At Cain's surprised look, he laughed. "I know you think of me as greedy, but—"

"You *are* greedy."

The Devil actually looked offended for a long moment, then he shrugged his shoulders. His lips crooked into a grin. "True." He rubbed his hands together. "That's why this is all the better.

Yes, numbers matter; but in the big picture, a number is just temporary. It can always be added to."

Cain shook his head in amusement. "Greedy, greedy, greedy."

It won him another smile. "Yes. But when all is said and done, I need something more than just a horde of tormented souls. I need to base my accomplishments on something a bit more substantial. Sure, we work hard, and every recruit counts—but numbers are just not enough."

Cain was lost. "What are you talking about? You want something on a larger scale? Something to make a statement while bringing in a big number of souls at the same time? Like mass destruction—a drought or nuclear holocaust?"

"Good ideas, but not quite what I was thinking. I mean we need to start focusing on quality. Finesse. Your ideas are too easy. Besides, those suggestions just collect already sold souls. I want to corrupt more. And I want to focus on quality. And something more."

"I'm not following you."

"There's a woman—"

"There are lots of women."

"Not like this one. She's smart. Brilliant. And so pitifully desperate. And also, she's on to something big. Something that will change the rules of our game should it fall into the wrong hands. Or the right ones."

"This is about that."

"Yes. You see, she's *this* close to finding the secret to life itself. To *eternal* life." The Dark One smiled; a slow, wicked expression that would have sent a chill through Cain had the fire of damnation not already burned him. "She thinks I can give it to her, but I can't. However, when she finds it on her own, you, dear boy, are going to convince her to give it to me."

Cain stepped from the dark shadows that filled the far corner of the living room of the high-rise apartment in downtown Chicago. Its large windows overlooked the river. The water below rippled beneath the light breeze, its surface reflecting the moon overhead. Light spilled through the glass, illuminating the apartment's interior.

Before him, a woman lay sprawled on a large white leather couch, her hair like dark silk spread out across a white satin throw pillow. Her features were passive, her breathing slow and easy. A half-empty bottle of champagne sat on the floor next to her.

Cain moved farther into the room, toward the woman as if drawn by an invisible hand. He imagined she stood before him, arms open and inviting, her body ripe and waiting. Wanting.

33

She would rise at any moment, strip off her clothes . . .

Inching closer, he reached out, eager to touch the woman's warmth, to soak it into himself. His fingers stopped just shy of her as he felt a cold, invisible grip on his wrist. The pressure tightened like a vise, sending through him a bolt of blinding pain.

It was the one bad thing about being a spirit: His senses were heightened, and so he felt everything more fiercely than a mere man. Pleasure *or* pain.

"Not yet." The Evil One's deep, smooth voice pushed past the terrible sensation of his grip. "First, you must help her find what she seeks."

"What are you talking about?" Cain managed, his lips pressed tight against the excruciating pain. It was too cold, too tight, too much to think . . .

"Remember. She's *this* close, but she isn't quite there yet. She needs you to help her find the final answer. She needs your hands, Cain. Your eyes. She needs you to see for her. Only after that can you begin your seduction."

"I'm not a scientist. I'm an incubus."

"One with a special talent. One I must use right now." The Evil One's voice crackled around him like firecrackers popping. "You will do this, Cain. I command it."

The pain around his wrist intensified until Cain had trouble seeing. Blackness edged his vision, grew until the woman on the couch faded into a tiny pinpoint. He saw nothing; he only felt the pain, the coldness.

"I know you want her, but you must help her first. *Then* you can have her."

"I . . ." He struggled to speak. "I can't . . ."

"You can, and you will. Fail me and you will step into the shadows, never to return. I'll take away this punishment you so greatly cherish. There'll be nothing to take your mind off the past. I'll just leave you down in Hell forever."

The words penetrated Cain's haze and filled him with a rush of dread unlike any he'd ever felt. He nodded, for he couldn't imagine an eternity in the Fire. This punishment was his chance to redeem himself. He wanted to make amends, not float around in the nothingness with only his thoughts, his regrets, his past to consume him.

He couldn't do that.

He *wouldn't*.

With that resolution came instant release from the pain. The coldness faded, and he found himself standing before his prey. She was so close, yet so far away considering the conditions to which he'd just agreed.

As if he'd had a choice.

"No, you can't touch her yet," the Evil One said. "Not directly. But you can give her sweet dreams." He glanced toward the windows. "For a short time, anyhow. Mind yourself, though.

35

The sun will be up soon, and the shadows will fade."

Cain nodded. He watched as the Evil One faded into the darkness that clustered in the far corner of the room, then he turned his attention back to the sofa. Since he couldn't touch, he contented himself with watching the woman on it for a long moment. He drank in her every detail, starting at the top of her head and the long, dark hair that spilled over the pale couch, and ending with her dainty toes.

Moonlight bathed her features in an ethereal light, made her nose seem even more delicate, her cheekbones higher and sculpted. He could see the faintest impressions near her mouth, and he knew that if he were to see her smile she would have dimples. Her full, sensuous lips parted as she made a small, mewling sound, as if lost in a disturbing dream.

He could easily have found out exactly what troubled her if this had been a typical seduction. He would close the distance between them and sink inside her, into her body, her thoughts. As a spirit, he had the power of possession, which he often used to learn his subjects' desires. He couldn't read their minds the way the Evil One could—as a mere incubus, he didn't have such power—but he could see their thoughts when he possessed their physical bodies.

Though only for a short time.

Possession was extremely taxing, for one spirit had to suppress another for the duration. It was a constant struggle. No spirit would willingly bow to that of another; it went against human nature. Eventually, he was always forced out.

Even if the host body wouldn't win eventually, anyway, Cain would have been limited by things other than its natural push to drive him out. He had been around a long, long time without his own physical form. While he was strong at night, his spirit weakened during the day. He always had to give up his hold before dawn. Yet what he had was always plenty of time to uncover the deepest, darkest, most erotic desires of whatever woman he possessed.

He sighed. This time, however, he had to settle for a whole different plan of attack. To start, he would stimulate his prey's senses enough to incite a much more pleasurable dream than the one she was currently having.

He saw a tear slide from the corner of her eye and wend a path down her cheek, and it was all he could do to resist the urge to reach out and catch the drop with his fingertip.

No touching.

Not yet.

He forced his attention away from the woman's face to the smooth expanse of her throat, the frantic pulsebeat at its base, to the neckline of her white cotton T-shirt. Then lower still. Her nipples pebbled beneath his examination, pushing against the material of her shirt. The areolas made pale, mouthwatering shadows. The thin fabric grew taut, outlined those turgid tips, and he swallowed.

His attention continued downward. Her skirt's hemline had ridden up to reveal a skimpy pair of red thong panties. The color was a direct contrast to her soft white skin. A few wisps of dark hair peaked through the lace pattern, and Cain's heart hammered a furious rythmn.

"No touching."

The Evil One's voice echoed through him, and he drew in a deep, shaky breath. Not that air sustained him in any way; he wasn't a man anymore, merely the image of a man. Even so, old habits were hard to break, and the action helped him gather control.

Control?

The notion was crazy, yet it was something he was going to have to exercise throughout this assignment, until he helped his prey make her precious discovery so he could get on with the real task.

In the meantime, he leaned down and whispered in her ear.

38

Chapter Four

"I want to touch you."

The deep voice floated into Sophie's thoughts and drew her from the darkness where she'd been locked away, frightened and lonely. Always lonely.

"Open your eyes."

She did as she was told and suddenly the blackness softened, faded, and she saw him. Her breath caught. The man looming over her was tall and handsome with long, flowing blond hair that fell past broad shoulders. She'd never seen him before, yet she felt as if she had known him forever.

She didn't know him, though, and she should be afraid. But it wasn't fear that pumped her full of adrenaline, made her chest heave as her breathing sped up. It was excitement.

Hunger.

Someplace in the back of her mind, Sophie knew she shouldn't be feeling such things. Even if she knew this man, now was not the time for sex. Not now, when she needed to concentrate. She needed to focus on her experiments, on keeping her depression at bay long enough to figure out solutions. But then the man leaned down, and she felt the slow glide of his long, silky hair, and her thoughts faded into a rush of feeling. Of sensation. Of desire.

"I'm not just going to touch you," the man said. "I'm going to touch you slowly, stroke you, prime you."

She glimpsed something that looked like fire flare in his bright green eyes a moment before her own closed and her head lolled back. Her senses were swamped by an incredible sensation. Those long, silken strands of hair feathered across her stomach, made her clench in anticipation. Her lower body responded eagerly to the promise of his words.

Pleasure.

Pure, mind-consuming pleasure.

The man touched her cheek first, just a barely felt caress that sent tingles through her body. The stroke proceeded down the slope of her neck, over her collarbone, to the fullness of her breasts. The fingers circled her nipples, teased and taunted until she moaned. Then the warmth of his mouth closed over one aching nipple and he sucked as if drinking in sweet nectar. She arched against him.

Suddenly, the man's touch grew bolder, fiercer, more fiery. It wasn't just his fingertips that made contact with her bare skin, but his full hands. They trailed down her stomach, beneath her panties, to delve into the slick folds between her legs. He stroked there, wringing a long, loud moan from her as he slid a finger deep, deep inside.

She tightened around him, relishing the feel as he pushed in and out in a delicious rhythm. He slipped a second finger inside.

Faster and faster, he began to push.

Harder and harder . . .

Deeper and deeper . . .

"Yes!"

Sophie's voice rang out and pushed past the frantic beat of her own heart. Her eyes snapped open and she glanced down to see her T-shirt ridden up over her breasts. Her panties pooled at her ankles, her bottom bare against the cool leather of the couch.

Dawn cracked open the sky beyond the windows, allowing just enough light for her to see beyond a doubt that she was alone. There was no tall, dark stranger looming over her. No fiery green eyes bright with passion. No silky blond hair trailing over her skin, teasing her senses, promising her a pleasure more intense than any she'd ever experienced.

There was nothing but an empty room still

41

bathed in shadows. All was dark and quiet. Peaceful. As if nothing out of the ordinary had just happened and Sophie Louise Alexander hadn't just had the hottest, wettest, most erotic dream of her entire life.

But this time she'd done more than merely fantasize. She'd been an active participant, pulling her own T-shirt up, pushing her undies down.

That was the only plausible explanation. She'd obviously touched herself, teased, primed her own body for the fantasy lover her mind had created. Even now she ached and throbbed. His fingers had been so deep and full inside of her.

But there'd been no *him*.

She'd been solo, with nothing but a vivid fantasy fueled by her own lust.

Lust?

It had been so long since she'd felt such a thing that it was a wonder she could even remember the concept. She hardly slept, much less dreamed of anything or anyone. When she did, they were dark, desperate dreams of death and destruction. She always woke to find herself drenched in sweat, her heart pounding from fear . . .

Never from lust.

At least, not in the past few years since her normal life had turned upside down; not since the tragic news that her sweet Kara, her godchild, was dying of leukemia.

Sophie closed her eyes and guilt washed through her. It was a feeling she had often now as she tried to go about her daily routine and maintain some sense of normalcy.

She tried to remain perky for Kara's sake. At seven, her goddaughter's comprehension of life and death was somewhat limited. She knew she was sick, but she didn't understand with just how grave an illness.

And the little girl was an inspiration in herself. However tired and frail, she still laughed at cartoons, played with Barbie dolls and giggled about the Backstreet Boys just like any other girl her age. She embraced each day with a child's usual optimism, excited to see the sun rise, to hear the birds sing and to watch her favorite TV programs.

She *lived*, with no thought to her future, or lack of one.

Sophie intended to see Kara stay that way, which was why she didn't have time for such lusty dreams. She had to stay focused. To think of Kara first and foremost. To think of the cure.

She tried to conjure her goddaughter's image, but she couldn't see past the memory of the handsome stranger with his deep green eyes and full, sensuous lips.

Geez, what a mess. Obviously, all those years of indulging her vices had finally caught up with her. While she'd always used caution, particularly with men, she wasn't exactly used to abstinence; this dream had been her body's biological needs manifesting themselves.

Talk about hard up. She tossed her shaky legs over the edge of the couch to the floor and stumbled toward the bathroom.

Flicking on the shower, she peeled off her clothes and dove beneath its icy spray. For several long, furious heartbeats, she simply stood there, letting the cold water calm her, until her teeth were chattering and she could actually think beyond the dream to the night before.

The candles and the spell and . . .

Ugh.

She'd obviously inhaled too many fumes from the endless experiments she'd done over the years. That, or she hadn't been able to hold the champagne she'd drunk. The memories she had were so crazy that she didn't even think she'd be able to imagine them drunk.

It was probably both. Fumes *and* booze. That was the only explanation for what she remembered. What she imagined she remembered.

With that explanation in mind, she climbed out of the shower, donned her robe and walked into the living room. Here she'd seen the Devil standing the night before.

The *Devil*.

Sure, and she was meeting Tinkerbell at the local Starbucks for a cappucino later this morning.

She'd been deranged and drunk. If there

wasn't a God—and she felt fairly certain there wasn't considering the injustice in the world—then a devil was certainly out of the question. No ultimate good, therefore little need for an ultimate evil. She'd simply imagined the entire episode. It had been a desperate daydream inspired by Dr. Stevens's phone call about Kara's remission.

Good news—or it would have been if she hadn't heard the same words less than one year ago. That reprieve had only lasted a few short months. Then they'd faced more chemotherapy, more experimental drugs advocated by the specialist, more pain.

No. She understood what had happened last night. While she'd been happy to have Kara in remission again, she hadn't shaken her fear that it wouldn't last. Not really. She'd tried to celebrate, to focus on the positive instead of the negative. But with each sip of champagne, she'd felt her anxiety mount along with her fear.

Remission was almost more terrifying than the sickness. It brought fear—fear of embracing the joy, only to lose it again. Fear of losing Kara for good this time.

She couldn't, she wouldn't simply wait and pray. The remission wasn't a certainty, but it did buy her time to actually *do* something to help. And so last night she'd killed herself going over possibilities, doing her damndest to for-

45

mulate a plan of action. A way to go faster with her research. To beat the odds.

But there was still too much to do. Too many possible combinations to test in such a short time.

She was closer, of course, than she'd been six months ago when the idea had first struck. It had come during a brainstorming session at the cosmetics company where she headed the research and development team. Her CEO had wanted a new youth cream. Something cutting edge.

Most scientists would have looked at ways to improve an existing product. To make the effects last longer or the cream smell better. The active ingredient currently being used dulled the effects of aging; it restored calcium and vital nutrients to the cells that were lacking and improved their condition, albeit temporarily. But Sophie had contemplated a different approach than a simple makeover. Motivated by the need to help Kara, she'd looked at the project with a completely different perspective. One with a two-fold purpose: help a sick child *and* boost her company's flagging sales. No problem—if she could find an active ingredient that didn't just invigorate the dying cells, but preserved the living ones.

A real youth cream, no cheap gimmick.

Forever Young.

The concept had seemed far-fetched to everyone at her company, but Sophie had done background work. She had the cell's present state. All that was left was to find a stabilizing compound to maintain the effect for more than five minutes, one that didn't interfere with the active ingredient. One that didn't melt skin instead of preserve it.

Now, after months of work, she felt so close to success.

But close wasn't good enough.

It wouldn't buy Kara one more precious day. Only her perfected formula would do that, and so she'd been in a race against time. The remission gave her a little more, but she knew in her heart it was only a little.

One month and twenty-nine days.

She needed to go faster. The work was exhausting, the possibilities too many. She needed a way to speed things up. Everyone thought she was crazy, but she knew she could do this; she believed she could win.

And then, after that champagne and her desperation last night, an answer had presented itself in the form of that old cheesey horror flick. An insane, bizarre, impossible answer. Which she realized even more now. The movie had been fictitious.

Make-believe.

Wishful thinking.

If only the answer she sought could be acquired as easily as by casting a quick spell, the

47

cost as minimal as her soul. To give her god-daughter a full life of days and smiles, a real chance, she would gladly trade eternity.

As if her thoughts conjured the small girl, a soft, familiar voice sounded behind her. "I made you a picture."

Sophie turned to see Kara standing in the living room doorway wearing her favorite pink Barbie nightgown, her feet bare, her toenails painted a bright shade of pink, her platinum blond hair mussed from sleep. The child carried a sheet of paper in one hand and her favorite purple marker in the other.

Smiling, Sophie plopped down on the sofa and patted the cushion next to her. Her god-daughter settled there and handed over the sheet of paper.

Sophie stared at a green pasture dotted with daisies. A pig stood in the center holding a bouquet, a smile on his face.

"Arnold loves flowers," Kara declared. "Daisies are his favorite. I'm going to have an entire garden of them when we move to the country. If we *ever* move to the country."

"The country" referred to the small Texas town and picture-perfect farmhouse where Kara had spent the first three years of her life.

"Soon, sweetie." Sophie longed for those green pastures and the calm, peaceful quiet almost as much as Kara. She, too, wanted to get away from the city, to Gruene, Texas, and a simpler way of life.

But her goddaughter's desperation to move was slightly different than Sophie's; it was fueled by an eagerness to be close to her mother's grave. To walk through the house where she'd been raised by her loving parents, parents who'd given up their fast-paced, high-powered business careers in order to focus on her, their budding family.

Sophie had been shocked when her best friend, Gwen, had told her about the decision to move to Gruene. Gwen had thrived on pressure and power just like her husband. Just like Sophie's parents.

Until she'd discovered she was pregnant.

Then Gwen's thoughts had quickly shifted from her own health to that of her child's; just like that, her priorities had changed. She and her husband, Ed, had both agreed that they wanted their daughter to have grass rather than concrete for a backyard. They'd packed up and left Chicago.

The move had been hard for Sophie and Gwen, but the pair had been best friends for over ten years; a relocation couldn't end such friendship. They'd kept in touch through daily phone calls and frequent visits. It had been on just such a visit—Sophie had flown to Texas for Kara's third birthday—when Gwen and Ed had died in a tragic car accident. They'd driven into town to pick up Kara's birthday cake and never come home.

The couple's Last Will and Testament had named Sophie as Kara's guardian and estate trustee. Hardly a surprise. Gwen had said on more than one occasion that she wanted Sophie to take care of Kara if anything were to happen. She'd even made Sophie promise.

Likewise, she'd promised to do the same for Sophie should Sophie ever marry and have children.

No, there had been little choice when Gwen and Ed died. Despite her fear at being a parent, Sophie had stepped up to the plate. She loved Kara as much as she'd loved Gwen, so she had packed the little girl up and brought her back to Chicago, to this high-rise apartment she'd purchased right after landing her position at Beyond Beauty.

It was the first really responsible thing she'd ever done—at least by her parents' standards. Certainly her career had been a far cry from the grand Alexander tradition. Her parents researched and formulated plastics for the Space Shuttle, restructured fuel molecules to produce a faster, more efficient take-off. They used their adeptness at chemistry to better mankind, a legacy they'd wanted their daughter to continue.

Which was, of course, why Sophie had gone the opposite direction. Why she'd turned her attention to making frivolous cosmetics. Why she'd finally succeeded in getting herself permanently ostracized by her parents, why they didn't even know about Kara or their daughter's life.

They hadn't understood her occupational decision, just as they'd never understood anything she'd done while growing up. Why she stayed out past curfew or constantly challenged them with her behavior.

The thing was, Sophie had never wanted their understanding. She'd wanted their support. Their affection.

Their love.

They'd never given it, and so she had been secretly pleased at their reaction to her career choice. She liked making frivolous cosmetics, and she liked that her job's superfluity was a stick in her parents' craw.

Usually.

Now, however, she was as serious about her chemistry as they had ever been, searching as she did for something that truly would benefit mankind. And it was all for a small, petite blonde with a bright smile and the bluest eyes Sophie had ever seen.

Kara.

It was ironic that what the girl wanted and what the girl needed were at such odds, as were the things that Sophie needed and wanted. Now, Sophie could move to Texas and be happy. Way back when, before her goddaughter had taken sick, moving hadn't been a consideration. She'd fought too hard for her job as chief chemist, worked too many hours to move up the ladder in research and development—not to mention she finally earned a substantial salary. She hadn't wanted to trade that all in for cow patties and record-breaking heat.

That's what her life had been about back then—her career and all that it involved—prestige and money.

But illness had a way of rearranging a person's priorities. Now, Sophie found herself as eager to move as the little girl. She had grown tired of this city: the congestion, the traffic, the fast pace.

She wanted to slow down.

To breathe.

To *live*.

One day at a time.

Unfortunately, such a move wasn't possible at the moment. Not with her research going on and Kara's treatment.

"We could find a new doctor in Texas," Kara said as if reading her thoughts. "A bunch of new doctors. As many as I need."

"We could, but they aren't anywhere near Gruene. Texas Children's Hospital is all the way in Houston, and Dr. Stevens said it wouldn't be advisable to start over with a bunch of new people who aren't familiar with your case, sweetie. We have to be near the experts, and that means living here for a little while longer."

"Just a little while?"

"If I have anything to say about it."

"When we move, can I have a pig?"

"How about a dog?"

"I want a pig. A big, fat pink pig."

"You've been watching *Green Acres* again, haven't you?"

"It's my favorite show, and I love Arnold. He's the cutest." The little girl leaned back and closed her eyes, as if imagining the future. A smile curved her lips. "Actually, I need two pigs. Two big, fat, pink pigs. If I had just one, he might get lonely."

Kara understood loneliness too well. Being sick had pulled her out of school far too many times, had kept her cooped up, unable to talk or play with other kids her age. She'd longed for a playmate during those times, but she'd had only Sophie—who'd been busy trying to balance her career with being a mom—and Snowball.

Sophie sighed and watched as the small kitten made its way over to the sofa. Leaning down, she scooped up the ball of white fluff and deposited it in her goddaughter's lap.

Kara opened her eyes and cuddled the feline. "That way, Arnold the First could play with Arnold the Second while I play with Snowball." The cat meowed as if in agreement, and Kara cuddled her even closer. "Snowball and I are best friends, aren't we?"

53

The comment brought to mind a memory of Sophie's own best friend. A sudden rush of tears burned her eyes. She moved to wipe the wetness away, but she wasn't fast enough. Kara saw her and her smile faded.

"Why are you crying, Aunt Sophie?"

"I'm not crying, sweetie. I just got something in my eye."

Kara frowned. "We aren't supposed to lie." Her expression softened. "And we're not supposed to cry anymore either, remember? We should only smile from here on out because we have a lot to smile about." She beamed. "I'm getting a lot better."

"I know you are." Sophie blinked back her tears and took a deep breath. She gave Kara her biggest grin and reached out to tickle her feet. The girl burst into a fit of giggles.

"We're going to smile and laugh until our faces are swollen and our sides hurt," Sophie went on, relishing the girl's high-pitched squeals. "And we're not going to cry again, or even think about crying."

"Can we eat before our faces get too swollen?" Kara finally managed to ask between giggles. "Please?"

Sophie stopped tickling her. "Name your poison."

"Pancakes."

"Pancakes it is."

"And sausage."

"A girl after my own heart."

"And syrup. Lots of syrup."

"Now you're talking."

"And whipped cream. And chocolate chips."

"Hold it. This is breakfast, not dessert. Your teeth will rot."

"So?"

"So, you have to take care of them. Not to mention, too much sugar is bad for you."

"Okay. Five spoonfuls of whipped cream and a half cup of chocolate chips."

"One spoonful of whipped cream and no chocolate chips." The girl's face fell, and Sophie had the sudden urge to give in.

It was the Last Supper urge, or so the people in the counseling group she'd gone to a few times liked to call it. Parents of terminally ill children tended to forego normal routine in the face of such grave illness—which, unfortunately, was the worst thing they could do. Sick kids needed to feel normal. They needed routine. They needed hope.

They needed a miracle cure.

Desperation gripped Sophie and pulled her from the couch. "Come on, kiddo. I'll cook, and then you can help me with dishes."

"Can I wash?"

"If you promise to be very careful." The response earned a wide smile. "And no dumping the entire bottle of dishsoap into the sink this time. We don't need that many bubbles for a few dirty plates."

Kara gave a salute. "You're the boss."

The pair spent the next hour going through their usual morning routine: breakfast, dishes, medication.

Once everything had been put away, Sophie helped Kara pick out school clothes, then she left the girl to get dressed while she went into her own bedroom to get ready for the day. The sooner she got to the lab, the sooner she could get to work on her formula.

She was halfway down the hall when the phone rang.

"Hello?"

"How is Kara this morning?" Dr. Stevens's voice floated over the line the way it did every day at this time.

"She's well. She's up and around. Playing and eating and smiling."

"Good," the man said. But the word was laced with an audible amount of doubt.

Dr. Chris Stevens was one of the leading pediatric cancer specialists in the country, and head of cancer research at Chicago Memorial Hospital. He'd spearheaded many treatment programs, including the new laser chemotherapy that Kara had recently undergone. He knew everything about the disease and everything about the various treatments and therapy.

Yet while Sophie respected him, she didn't really like him. He had tended to be very pessimistic when giving Kara's prognosis, leaving very little room for hope. Sophie had begun to associate him with the disease.

It didn't help her feelings for him that, as his reputation maintained, he was very seldom wrong. He had a perfect track record when it came to assessing sick patients. He could name each specific cancer and its outcome with an alarming accuracy. The talent had earned him national aclaim among medical professionals and the nickname of Sure-shot Stevens, but it hadn't endeared him to Sophie.

"I wouldn't get my hopes up if I were you."

His words echoed through her head: advice he'd given her when he'd made the initial diagnosis, then again after the first round of chemotherapy, and again just yesterday.

"Don't celebrate just yet."

Sophie found herself being optimistic, just to counter Dr. Stevens's pessimism. "She looks really good. I think the chemo really worked this time."

"I wouldn't take it to the bank just yet. We always see a marked improvement once the side-effects subside, but then that fades. Especially for patients with this type of cancer. It's often too aggressive to slow down for long."

"But it has stopped before. There have been cases, haven't there?"

"Very few."

57

"But a few is better than none. Kara could be one of the few."

He didn't comment. Instead, he let his silence answer.

"Don't let her overdo it," he finally said. "I know she feels almost one hundred percent, but she's not. The cancer could still be there."

As if Sophie needed to be reminded.

"If it's still there, it's standing still," she proposed.

"For now."

"Has anyone ever called you the poster boy for optimism?"

"It's not a question of being optimistic, Sophie. It's about being realistic. Things are calm now, but that doesn't mean they'll stay that way. I just don't want to see you disappointed when and if this hiatus ends. It's hard enough on the kids as it is, but it's worse when the parents refuse to see the truth and help their children deal with it."

"I *see* the truth. I just think Kara needs hope, too. And that's what I'm trying to give her: real hope."

"Good things often come to an end."

"Maybe not this time."

"Meaning?"

"Meaning I'm working on something that I think might help."

"What?"

She wasn't sure why she didn't blurt out the

details of *Forever Young*. Probably because she'd mentioned her research to him before—she'd even hinted at the possibility that if an anti-aging cream could be developed for skin, what was to say that it couldn't be developed for other organs and tissue—and he hadn't paid much attention. He'd just written off her comments as the wild hopes of a desperate woman. As did most of the scientists she talked to.

But when she could show them solid proof . . .

"I know you're referring to the typical pattern of this type of cancer, Dr. Stevens. But there's always the exception. Maybe Kara will be different. Maybe she'll be the case that everyone reads about in the next medical journal."

"Maybe," he agreed. But there wasn't much of a *maybe* in his voice. He didn't believe. He wouldn't believe, because he made his living at believing in his own thoughts and opinions, and nothing else figured in.

"Make sure you bring her in for bloodwork on Friday," he said after a long silence. "I want to check her levels."

"She'll be there," Sophie assured him. Then she hung up the phone and went into her bedroom.

If she put her mind to it, she *could* do it. She would find the missing ingredient. That's what she told herself as she pulled a blouse and slacks from the closet. She let her robe slide to the ground, retrieved her bra, and turned toward the mirror. With intense concentration, she could do this. Even if she had to work every hour of every day of every week. She simply had to think. To test. To—

As she turned, she caught her reflection in the mirror. Her attention riveted on her exposed shoulder. Air lodged in her chest.

It couldn't be. Last night had been wishful thinking, the product of a drunk and desperate imagination.

No. It was real.

The thought took root as her fingertip traced the vivid red mark on her shoulder. It resembled a pair of horns. Wasn't that the exact pattern that she recalled the Devil following the night before with his razor-sharp fingernail?

She swallowed convulsively.

Denial raged fierce and furious in her brain; her heart pumped faster and made her body tangle. She had to be hallucinating. Spells and such didn't really work. Only in the movies or in books. And she'd been tipsy from champagne, enacting a scene from a silly Sci-Fi Channel re-run. This stuff didn't happen in real life.

But even as she told herself what a lunatic she was, she couldn't deny the mark. It was proof that she'd really and truly promised her soul to the Devil.

As that thought settled in, a wave of new fear

welled up inside her. There would be no turning back, no re-thinking her decision and bailing on it.

Not that I would, she told herself. No matter how afraid I am. Far greater than her fear was a new hope that bubbled inside her. Yes, she'd offered to sell her soul, all right, but for a worthwhile cause. For Kara.

Chapter Five

He knew everything about her.

He knew the exact street address of the apartment building where she lived on the tenth floor in uptown Chicago.

He knew the dwelling itself, from the front and rear elevators to the emergency stairwell located at the very back. There were two fire escapes and three different exit doors on the ground floor. There were four different doormen who split the twenty-four-hour weekdays, with a fifth who filled in on the weekends and holidays.

Sam. That was the name of the current doorman, whose face filled the small television screen for a split second before the picture widened and Sophie's image appeared. The surveillance tape played on, showing Sam hold the door open for her. Sophie exited the building and turned left, headed up the street to her office building. Three blocks, to be exact.

He knew the exact type of donut she would order as she stopped off at the Krispy Kreme on the way: chocolate-glazed with nuts. Sometimes she went for the regular glazed, but only when they were out of chocolate.

He knew she ate her hamburgers with mustard instead of mayo, and that she never went out for lunch but preferred to order from the deli in the lobby of her office building. Twelve-thirty. That's what time she ate. Afterwards, she visited the ladies room on the fifth floor—the level where her lab was located—to freshen up. She brushed her teeth and freshened whatever lipstick she wore. If she wore any. She didn't have much of an affinity for makeup. She was very low-key. Simple. Often, she just brushed and finger-combed the long dark hair she always wore in a loose ponytail.

He knew how mussed her hair looked when she rolled off her red satin sheets, when she crawled between them in the first place. Lately, she'd been nodding off on the couch or at her desk . . . or sometimes on the sofa in the far corner of her lab.

She flipped on MTV late at night whenever she took a break from the report she always brought home from the lab. She listened to

Aerosmith after a productive day at work, and George Strait when things weren't going so well. She loved Victoria's Secret catalogs and occasionally ordered online. She wore scented body lotion and washed her hair with Pantene.

Yes, he knew *everything* about Sophie Alexander.

Because he watched.

And waited.

"So, how close are we?"

Before Sophie could respond to the tall, fortyish blonde who stalked the perimeter of the large marble conference table, the woman rushed on: "Miss International Beauty is only a little over two months away. Ten weeks to be exact."

Carol Hollister, president and CEO of Beyond Beauty Cosmetics stopped her pacing and leaned over to tap one long, red-lacquered nail against the tabletop. "We have to have *Forever Young* ready for FDA approval at least two weeks prior to the pageant. I've got friends in the department who can push the approval in time to film a few commercial spots, but that only gives us eight weeks."

"It'll be ready," David Hammond, marketing director and the only male seated at the table, assured her.

"That's right. We're ready to go with the slogan and a new theme song." Angela Marks, the ad liaison, held up a thick portfolio. "Ready and waiting."

Carol turned her hopeful gaze on Sophie. "Give me some good news. Please. Otherwise, I'm liable to head straight out of here and have a double chocolate mocha."

"The doctor said no caffeine!" called a petite redhead seated in the far corner. She paused in frantically scribbling the meeting notes and added, "None. As in, not even a sip."

"You're my secretary, Claire. Not my mother." At the girl's pointed stare, the CEO blew out an exasperated breath. "Okay, okay. No double mocha, even if it is bad news. Sophie?"

"It'll be ready." Sophie had a different deadline in mind, and it was less than eight weeks. Kara's reprieve had barely lasted two months the last time. This time, they were two days well and counting—and she intended to keep Kara healthy.

Her hand went to her shoulder where the Devil's marks burned on her skin. Heat seeped through the cotton of her white button-down blouse and warmed her fingertips.

Real.

She nodded. "We'll make it."

Carol gave her a pointed look. "I hope so, because Walker Skin and Beauty is spreading rumors that they've got something new that will blow anything we can come up with right out of the water. I would think they were just talking crap—they're experts at it—but after what happened with *Younger You*, I'm not so sure." The CEO shook her head. "I still can't understand how that bastard did it."

That bastard referred to Jeffrey Walker: president and CEO of Walker Skin and Beauty, Carol's archenemy and hated ex-husband. They'd gone through a bitter divorce five years prior. He'd cheated, she'd filed, and they'd both wound up in court.

The worst past was Jeffrey claiming a chunk of her company. Beyond Beauty was one of the leading cosmetic companies in the United States and a family legacy for Carol. Her grandfather had started the company and her father had continued it. Carol herself had left college to take over after a heart attack had taken her father out of the workplace. The youngest CEO in the business—she'd been twenty-two—Carol had worked like a dog over the next ten years while Jeffrey had played the social scene, spending his wife's money and making a fool of her.

And then, he'd managed through some legal technicality to convince a judge to give him a sizeable chunk of Carol's company. Unwilling to break up the Beyond Beauty, Carol had bought him out. He'd taken his money and started a rival concern that had been vying for Beyond Beauty's market share.

66

Last year, his company had passed hers by. It had taken the lead thanks to a big breakthrough scar-fading cream which contained a new complex that actually added elasticity to rough scar tissue to give it a newer, more pliable appearance.

Sophie's invention.

Over one year later, Sophie still didn't understand what had happened. She'd spent six months doing research and testing to formulate the new Elasticine. Just as she'd handed it over to the legal department to pursue patent approval, Walker Skin and Beauty had exploded onto the market with their own version: a compound that, under study, was virtually identical to her own—right down to the the active ingredient.

Carol had been ready to kill the entire ad campaign, determined not to release the product and look like a copycat, marketing and budget constraints had convinced her otherwise. *Younger You* had hit the shelves to recoup its investment. And it had done just that, with a nice profit to boot.

For Carol, however, success wasn't based on dollars and cents. In terms of innovation, she'd taken a backseat for the first time in her professional career—and to none other than her hated ex. It was not an acceptable situation. She immediately turned the company's concentration to this new product, to this new ad campaign scheduled to debut during Miss International Beauty, the Super Bowl of pageants. She'd been determined to regain her industry standing, and Sophie's idea for a new anti-aging cream had been the way. Now, however, they were down to the wire, and Carol seemed terrified.

Sophie knew the feeling, but she had made up her mind not to let it distract her. She couldn't afford, either professionally or personally, to lose focus. She had her own stake in this, her own need to speed things up.

Her shoulder throbbed in response to the thought, a reminder that she'd promised her soul to the Devil in return for an answer. Carol might breathe easier if she knew that. Or, she might not.

Sophie turned to the CEO. "I'm almost done," she said. Her voice was full of determination. "I'll make the deadline."

"Good." Carol blew out a final breath and sank down into the large leather chair at the head of the table. "We'll step up security." She made a few notes on her legal pad and looked around the room. "I don't want anything to happen this time. No bugs, no spies, no leak." She shook her head. "It had to be a leak. That's the only way Jeffrey could have known. The only way he could have gotten that formula. If someone here told him."

"Do you really think he could get someone on

68

the inside here to divulge information?" David asked.

"I wouldn't put anything past Jeffrey. He's determined to ruin me. If he can't spend my money, he'll make sure I don't make any more. He'll steal it if he can, destroy it if he can't."

"That's how he was during our marriage," Carol went on. "If he couldn't have a particular designer suit, he was always intent on making sure no one else bought it. One time he spilled ink all over this one-of-a-kind Armani that he wanted. I wouldn't fork over the dough, so he ruined it right there in the shop when the salesman wasn't looking. Needless to say, I ended up paying for it."

She turned to Angela Marks. The attractive redhead was clad in a black pin-striped suit, and she sat across from Sophie. She was in her late twenties, and she had both a degree in marketing and a reputation as a hot commodity down at Smitty's, the local bar and grill located on the first floor of the office building. She had a car salesman mentality—oily and determined—and a body guaranteed to cinch any deal. Sophie had never really cared for her, but she respected that the woman knew how to play the sales game and always won.

"Make sure you talk to maintenance about changing the security codes," Carol told Angela. "I want them re-programmed every week until this product goes to patent."

"Don't you think that's a little James Bond-ish? We're not talking some cutting edge nuclear weapon. This is only a face cream."

"This is your job. It's mine. It's all of ours." Carol let the seriousness of her words sink in, then smiled; her worried expression gave way to determination. "And this will be Jeffrey's ass. Anybody can come up with one breakthrough product. What makes success is consistent innovation, and that's what we have. *Forever Young* will prove that."

"You're the boss." Angela shrugged, gathering up her purse and cup of latté. The others around the table followed suit.

Sophie reached for her briefcase. Carol stopped her with a hand on her arm. "Keep me updated, Sophie. This has to work."

"It will," Sophie vowed, more for her own reassurance than Carol's. There was more at stake than a little corporate rivalry, here. This was life and death. This was life *instead* of death. And Sophie meant to succeed, even though it meant losing her soul.

"Cain!"

The cry, so fierce and desperate, pushed its way through the consuming darkness, calling to him the way it always did.

"Help me. Please!"

He tried to ignore the words, but the voice that spoke was too familiar, too precious, and it drew him from the nothingness. Far in the distance he saw a pinpoint of light that grew larger as the voice became louder.

"I need you, Cain!"

The darkness released him, thrusting him into the shadows that crowded the underground chamber of an old castle. Thick walls surrounded him. Stones dug into the soles of his bare feet.

He blinked, fighting to see, but it was still too dark. Suddenly, flames flared and candles flickered; the smell of true desperation filled his nostrils. A cold fist tightened inside him, and he knew he was about to see his worst fear realized.

He saw her then, on the opposite side of the chamber. She knelt, her head tilted back, her gaze fixed on the man who held a handful of her white-blond hair. Her cheeks were slicked with tears, her eyes wide with fear. She was completely naked save the coarse rope that bound her hands and feet, and the beefy fingers that threaded through her hair.

"A fine lass ye be," her attacker said. "Ah, fine, indeed. Such a shame ye must die."

"No!"

Cain's own voice echoed around him, but it was as if no one heard. As if he didn't really exist, the scene kept unfolding.

Tremors shook the blonde's helpless body as the fingers in her hair tightened. Her head arched back further, her slender neck pale in the candlelight.

71

"No!" Cain's voice rang out again—but this time it was as if she heard.

The woman's head craned around; her gaze locked with his. The candleflames that surrounded them reflected in the dark blue pools of her eyes. Her desperate cry filled his head.

"Please!"

He tried to step forward, but the castle seemed to come alive. Arms extended, hands surrounded him, pushing and pulling, holding him back so that he could do nothing but struggle and watch.

A blade flashed with silver fire in the shadowy chamber. It rose. The woman's breath caught. Fresh tears beaded on her lashes and spilled down her creamy cheeks.

The blade struck. The woman's sobs faded into a choked gurgle as a sticky red burst forth; squirted, flowed over the meaty fingers that clamped around her throat.

The pain around Cain's own neck grew tighter, hands trying to choke the life out of him. He welcomed the sensation. Anything to put him out of his misery and end this nightmare.

His wife was dead. Blackness edged Cain's vision as he stared across the chamber at her lifeless body. Invisible fingers wrapped around his heart, squeezed and tore until only pieces remained. Then the blackness won out and he saw nothing.

But he could still hear.

The knife clattered to the ground. He heard the body being dragged away, dead weight scraping the stone floor. Booted footsteps mounted the stairs.

And he could not only hear. He still felt. Pain filled his gut, twisting and pulling until he couldn't even draw breath.

Guilt because he'd been too late.

His precious wife was dead.

"No!"

Cain forced his eyes open to the dim hallway of a large office building. He stood hidden in a corner, cloaked in shadow.

For now he would conceal himself. Until night set in completely and the darkness grew. He would grow along with it, his energy growing with the approach of the Witching Hour.

Of course, he wasn't a witch, but his power and his senses heightened the same way theirs did. He assumed it was because he served the same dark master. Thus, for now, he had to wait.

He forced his heart back to its normal rhythm and tried to focus on his surroundings. The vision he'd just seen haunted him whenever daylight ruled and he was forced into the darkness to take refuge.

The days seemed endless because of it, and he knew that he couldn't endure an eternity of such—lost in the blackness, with nothing but the visions to fill his time.

No.

He had an assignment to complete.

Penance to pay.

And nothing would stop him.

He obviously wasn't interested in another soul.

Sophie stared into the small bathroom mirror that hung over the sink in the first-floor ladies' room at Beyond Beauty, trailing her fingertips over the fiery red marks on her shoulder.

Horns. They were still there, still a reminder of last night and the deal she'd made.

Some deal.

She'd spent the entire day in her lab, hovering over a petrie dish. She'd studied various combinations of twenty-four stabilizers, fully expecting each combination to be *the* one. The answer. Kara's cure. Wasn't that what the Devil had promised? What *had* he promised?

All she knew was, all day and not one successful experiment.

Her computer listed 30,000 likely combinations at varying amounts of each stabilizing compound—of which she'd tested three. At the rate she was going, it would be thirty years before she tried them all. And, of course with her luck, number 30,000 would be the correct formula.

Heat pulsed beneath her fingertips, and Sophie glanced at her reflection and the vivid mark.

It was *real*, all right. But was it a devil's mark? Maybe not.

Obviously not.

Perhaps she'd burned herself accidentally after those glasses of champagne, and she simply didn't remember. That, or she'd let the curling iron slip this morning. Or she'd pinched herself trying to get her collar free from her blouse. Or her electric blanket overheated last night.

All were plausible answers . . . except that she hadn't used her curling iron in ages. The blouse she was now wearing didn't have a collar. And she'd slept on the couch last night, a good fifty feet from her bedroom and her electric blanket. That wasn't to mention that nobody in Chicago slept with an electric blanket during the high heat of summer.

"It can't be real," she said to herself. "If it were real, a *real* devil's mark, then the deal would be real. You would be celebrating the discovery of a lifetime right now instead of standing in the bathroom talking to yourself."

"You don't get out enough. *That*'s why you're in the bathroom talking to yourself."

The voice drew Sophie around to find Angela Marks standing in the doorway. The redhead smiled—an expression that didn't quite touch her ice blue eyes—and pulled out a pack of Marlboro Lights.

"This is a non-smoking building."

"The building's not smoking. I am." Angela lit up and took a long, deep puff before walking up next to Sophie and staring into the mirror. "So, how did it go today?"

"Fine." Sophie busied herself washing her hands.

"Liar. You're having trouble, otherwise you would be out celebrating right now instead of talking to yourself in the ladies' room."

"I'm not having trouble," Sophie snapped.

"You don't have a patented formula," Angela returned.

"It's all about testing and elimination. I've got my core compound."

"That's true, but you don't have a patented formula. Do you?"

The urge to defend herself faded into a wave of desperation. Angela was right. She had no patented formula. Sophie let loose a frustrated sigh.

"That's what I thought. The whole project is a losing battle, isn't it?"

Sophie shook her head. "I'm on it. I'm close. A little more work and I'll be there."

"A little more work and you'll drop dead." Angela studied her, obviously referring to the dark circles that rimmed Sophie's eyes. "Are you getting any sleep at all?"

"I'm fine." Sophie averted her gaze and busied herself washing her hands.

"You're exhausted."

"I'm busy." And terrified. With last night's deal a pathetic dream, she was back to being on her own. Desperate. Alone. Putting all her energy into something that would fail her boss and not help her goddaughter.

No. Kara's still alive and breathing. She's had no new signs of the return of the disease.

For now.

She blinked back a sudden surge of tears.

"Are you crying?" Angela touched her on the shoulders.

"It's quitting time." Sophie turned and reached for the paper towels. She repeated, "It's quitting time. Shouldn't you be on your way home?"

"Are *you* going home?"

"I've got work to do. I can't leave." She blinked again at another swell of tears.

"Christ, you *are* crying."

"Would you just get out of here? I'm not crying. I'm just a little stressed."

"I know Carol's riding everyone, but you've got to keep things in perspective. This is only face cream."

Sophie shook her head. "I wish."

"What's that supposed to mean?" Angela stared at her and Sophie had the insane urge to blurt out her plan to find a formula for both Carol and the research and development department at Chicago Memorial Hospital. She wanted to explain how they would adapt it for proper medical use, how Kara would be the first test subject.

It was far-fetched—but wasn't it possible?

But who knew how long any of it would take? She had to move more quickly on her end.

"What's going on?" Angela asked again. "This thing is bigger, isn't it? Come on, Sophie. You can tell me."

Sophie shook her head. She wanted to speak up, but she wouldn't jeopardize her work. What if Carol was right? What if Jeffrey would destroy information that he couldn't steal? She wasn't going to tempt him with her hopes. The idea of his deliberate sabotage seemed a longshot, but it was certainly possible. And if he truly did have someone on the inside . . .

Sophie studied Angela's profile from the corner of her eye. Could the young woman be leaking information?

Maybe. Maybe not. Either way, Sophie wasn't taking any chances.

"Nothing's going on. We just need this face cream. We need something better than everyone else in the industry."

"Sure." The redhead eyed Sophie a minute more before she went on to another topic. "Look, I'm headed to Smitty's for a drink with some of the other marketers. Why don't you come with me? You can clue us in about your youth cream. Have a drink. Relax a little. Maybe some down time will rejuvenate you. Freshen your creativity. Maybe we marketers can think of something you scientists can't."

"No. I can't. I'm close, and the only thing that will see this project complete is more work." She wasn't going to give up yet. Her insane dream about the Devil's deal might be nothing but fanciful bunk, but she couldn't give up hope. She had to keep trying. She had to *do* something. To keep doing something. Otherwise, grief would overwhelm her. Worry. Fear. Hopelessness.

I don't need anybody.

Her mantra, spoken so often so long ago when she'd been fighting with her parents, echoed through her mind. She'd believed that statement to be the truth. She'd weaned herself on it throughout her adolescence. It had made her strong.

Gwen had helped her realize the need for others, though. Her friend had been shy and quiet and tame—a total opposite of Sophie's wild-child persona. She'd been a good girl where Sophie had been bad to the bone. Most of all, she'd been nice and sweet and pushy—and she'd kept asking questions, offering help, chipping at the hard exterior Sophie built up around herself until it finally crumbled. Gwen had gotten to know the real Sophie, and she'd been her true friend.

Yes, Sophie had once convinced herself that she was a hard-ass, that she didn't need anyone. But Gwen had helped her realize and admit that it was all just a show, a defense mechanism because her workaholic, career-driven parents had never given her the love she'd so desperately needed.

The truth had hit her slowly over the years as their friendship grew and she realized the joy of actually having someone care for her. And having someone she cared about, as well. She cared about her parents, but they didn't return that emotion. Thus, she'd eventually shut herself off. She'd retreated into her own destructive world, determined to get their attention even if she couldn't earn their love. All she'd earned herself was a ticket right out of her home, straight into a school for troubled girls.

Like her, everyone there had been defiant and independent. Everyone except for Gwen. Gwen had merely been scared and lonely—the same as Sophie under her I-don't-take-crap façade. They'd become roommates. They'd become friends. Gwen had been there for her, showed her how to love and how to acknowledge her weakness. When she'd passed on, her friend had left a piece of herself behind in the form of her daughter. Sophie owed Gwen for all those years of friendship, and she wanted desperately to pay her back by raising her daughter.

"Have a drink and then you can come back to work. Just get away for a few hours. It'll do you good."

Sophie turned and pinned Angela with a

stare. "I thought you were a marketer, not a psychiatrist."

"A marketing director *is* a psychiatrist. Knowing people is my job. I've got to pick their brains, figure out why they want what they want, why they do what they do, and what I can do to get them to want what I have." She smiled. "So, what can I do to convince you?"

"You're not going to be happy until you have me chugging beer with everybody else, are you?"

"I drink Cosmopolitans, honey. That, or martinis. But you're welcome to whatever. Rum and Coke. Club Soda, even. Or just a handful of peanuts. Anything, so long as you do something social that includes other people besides a lab assistant." The woman gestured widely. "The offer stands whenever you're ready. And if you want to talk about anything, look me up. I'm a good listener."

"Thanks," was all Sophie said. She waited for the door to swing shut behind Angela, then retrieved her cell phone from her purse and punched in her home number.

Kara's voice floated over the line after the first ring. "Where *are* you?" the child demanded.

"I'm working, sweetie."

"Come home. Now."

"Why?" Fear bolted through her. "Is something wrong? Are you feeling okay?"

"I'm fine. I just miss you."

"I miss you, too, but I'm working on a really important project. I have to do a few more things here before I leave. You go on to bed, and I'll see you in the morning. We'll have breakfast together."

"But I wanted us to eat pizza together. We'll have pepperoni. Your favorite."

Sophie laughed, then said, "*Mushroom* is my favorite. Pepperoni is yours."

The little girl giggled back. "You can pretend the pepperoni is mushroom. You're always telling me how good it is to use my imagination."

Sophie sighed, wanting to go home and embrace the child. "We'll pretend tomorrow night. I promise."

"Really?" At her reassurance, the little girl made a noise of acquiescence. "I guess so. I mean, it's not like I won't be hungry for pizza tomorrow night, too. I'm always hungry for pizza. And cookies. And cake. And ice cream."

Sophie grinned. "Why don't you have Beth build you a banana split." The young woman who watched Kara would be horrified at the nutritional value of the suggestion, but Sophie wanted to make her little girl happy.

"With whipped cream and chocolate chips?"

"If there's any left from breakfast."

"If there isn't, we can go to the store."

"Okay. Put Beth on, sweetie," Sophie said.

Kara agreed, then gave a loud smooching sound that Sophie had to reciprocate. Beth's voice sounded a few seconds later. "Where are you?"

"I've got to work late."

"Again? Kara and I were waiting dinner on you."

"I heard. You guys go on and eat. I've got to keep going here for a little while."

For Kara.

"When will you be home?"

"Actually, it'll be very late. Can you stay over? I know this is short notice, but this project is really close to deadline, and I need to devote every spare moment possible."

"No problem. There's no one waiting with bated breath for me at home."

"You and Calvin broke up?"

"Again," the younger woman acknowledged. "Whoever said that love was easy never met Calvin. I swear, he's the most temperamental man I've ever had the misfortune to date."

"What happened this time?"

"A Willie Nelson song came on the radio and I turned it."

"He broke up with you over that?"

"No, I broke up with him. He said that I had zero taste in music. He said Willie is a legend, and anyone with half a brain can appreciate that." She sighed loudly. "Can you imagine him telling me I only have half a brain?"

Sophie shook her head, surprised. "It sounds like he was just stating his opinion about Willie

Nelson. I'm sure he didn't mean that you were really missing anything upstairs. He loves you."

"Maybe," Beth agreed, her voice softer. "But it doesn't matter, because he hasn't called to say he's sorry. Until then, I'm officially solo and have no problem staying over."

"Thanks."

"You'd better be back for breakfast, though, or Kara's going to be upset. She already walked into the kitchen to plan a menu."

Sophie grinned. "I will. Tell her I'll see her tomorrow. First thing."

Tomorrow. That's why she was doing this: for all of Kara's tomorrows.

Because she'd promised Gwen.

She told Beth goodbye, punched the END button, and then turned back to the mirror. Letting out a deep, exasperated breath, she shoved a piece of stray hair that had come loose from her ponytail behind her ear, wiped at her watery eyes, and turned to leave the bathroom.

"Stop praying for miracles," she murmured as she pushed through the door.

The sun had already started to set, and shadows crowded the empty hallway outside. The only light came from a neon EXIT sign at the far end just to the right of the elevator.

"You're on your own tonight," she said to herself.

The way she had been her entire childhood and most of her adolescence.

Alone.

Lonely.

"Not tonight, Sophie." She heard the voice a heartbeat before she felt a hard, muscular body step up behind her. "Tonight, it's you and me."

Chapter Six

He wanted to touch her more than anyone he'd ever seen.

The urge hit Cain the moment Sophie Alexander whirled to face him, and he got his first full-on look at her.

He'd seen her last night, but she'd been lost in the throes of sleep. Unconscious and unaware. She was wide-awake now, staring directly back at him, and the effect filled him with a need more intense than any he'd ever felt. Women always shook him to the core and stirred every sense, but this was . . . different.

More intense.

More potent.

More consuming.

It was as if she were the first woman he'd ever had the pleasure of meeting.

As if she were the last he'd ever need to meet.

She looked so inviting: her green eyes bright, her full lips parted in surprise. Her chest heaved beneath the soft material of her blouse, pushing and stretching with each surprised gulp of air. She was of average height, but there was nothing average about her figure. Curves and dips cried out for the caress of his hand, the press of his lips, the flick of his tongue.

She smelled fantastic. Her scent, like sweet, ripe raspberries on a hot summer's day, drifted across the space between them and teased his senses. His nostrils flared, and his mouth watered.

He felt her warmth. Her body heat reached out to him, feeding the fire that already blazed deep inside.

Her demeanor was so feminine, so sexy— from her soft gasp when his gaze lingered a little too long on the top button of her blouse, to the sharp noise she made as his gaze locked with hers.

Her body went completely still.

Almost.

Had he not been more than a man, he wouldn't have known, but because of who he was, *what* he was, every sense that he possessed was heightened and attuned specifically to her.

Soon he heard only her, saw only her, felt only her—and he knew that Sophie's heart pounded in the same frenzied rhythm as his.

"I beg your pardon?" she said.

A grin tugged at the corner of his mouth. "You don't have to beg for anything, my sweet. I'm more than happy to oblige any request."

The statement seemed to stall her thought processes for a long moment, as if she couldn't quite digest the situation. He could see the thoughts racing through her head. The confusion. The wonder. The sadness.

Suddenly, he wanted to comfort her more than he wanted to touch or tease or tantalize.

Ridiculous.

"How do you know my name?" she finally asked, her words distracting him from the crazy urges bombarding him. She blinked, obviously fighting back tears which had been threatening since she walked out of the ladies room.

"I know a lot of things about you," he promised. His grin eased, and he stared deep into her eyes, willing her to relax. *It's okay, sweet Sophie. I'm not here to hurt you. I'm here to help.*

While he knew she couldn't read his mind any more than he could read hers, he felt that she was as attuned to his senses as he was hers. She would sense the calmness of his breathing, the steadiness of his heartbeat, the ease of his muscles, and her body would respond appropriately.

Her eyes went wide for an extended moment, as if she was surprised to have heard his words. Then her gaze narrowed and her body tensed. "Who are you, and how do you know my name?"

"My name is Cain." So much for calming her through a sensory connection.

The first woman . . . and the last. . . .

The thought struck him again because Sophie responded so differently than the other women had, as if his demonic charm didn't affect her as much.

Or, perhaps it affected her too much. Enough to force her protective instincts to kick in, to make her wary.

The last thought brought a smile to his face. He repeated, "I know your name just as I know many other things about you. You are a very smart lady. A chemist. You head the research and development department here at Beyond Beauty. You're working on a very important project right now. A major breakthrough."

The words seemed to induce some kind of recognition inside her, and her hand went to her purse. "Jeff sent you, didn't he?" She retrieved a cell phone. "I'm calling Security. Carol was right. A spy," she muttered as she backed away from him, punching buttons with every step.

Cain lifted a hand and closed his fingers, the

same way he would if he actually was going to touch her.

"You're in big troub—" The words stalled as her hand seemed to freeze in midair, an invisible force stopping her fingers from punching the last few buttons.

"I am not a spy."

"What . . . ?" Incredulous, Sophie stared at her hand as if it belonged to someone else. "How . . . ?"

"I am Cain," he told her again. "And I'm here to help you." He relaxed his fingers and her hand unfroze.

Her cell phone crashed to the floor, and she started to tremble. "I don't understand this," she said. She took another step back.

Cain advanced. "I'm here at your request—or don't you remember last night?"

The words seemed to strike a chord; recognition dawned and a spark lit her eyes. He wondered for a moment if she remembered her deal with the devil or the dream he himself had sent her.

"It's . . . you."

"Yes."

"But you—this morning—that was just—"

"A dream?" He shrugged, but was secretly pleased. She remembered *him*. "Perhaps, or maybe it was a vision. Have you the sight, sweet Sophie?"

"Sight?"

"Can you see into the future?" He stepped even closer.

She didn't back away; she simply stared at him, stunned, as if trying to grasp his words and the fact that she was facing the man from her most erotic imaginings.

"Can you see things that are going to happen? I can. That's why I am here. To use my sight to help you find your answers."

Suspicion flared in her eyes. "How do you know—"

"You made a deal," he explained, cutting her off. "Or was the dream I gave you so delicious you need a reminder of what came before?"

His gaze zeroed in on her shoulder where the fiery mark of his master lay covered. A moment's concentration and the button that had been straining slipped open. Her blouse parted. The silk slid down her soft, fragrant flesh just enough to reveal the tell-tale symbol burnt into her white skin. Cain licked his lips, and he knew by the sharp draw of air and the way Sophie stiffened that she felt the stroke against her flesh. Her confusion and fear faded into something much more potent.

Desire. He'd begun to instill it last night, and now his presence was recalling all of what she'd felt. He slowly smiled.

His own body trembled in response. His hands longed to reach out and pull Sophie hard and fast against him. He wanted to be deep inside her, to feel Sophie Alexander's hot, slick body pulse around him, to draw him deeper, more fully inside . . .

Slow down.

He fought for a deep breath and tried to regain control of his raging lust. He had to take this nice and easy. This seduction was different from all of the others. It wasn't about one hot night and an immediate surrender.

Why not? he wondered. The sooner the better, in order for him to move on to the next woman. But while he would have been satisfied to do just that, he'd been commanded to help this brunette find answers to something outside of the bedroom. He couldn't simply defy the Evil One and risk eternal oblivion. He had to play this seduction out as planned, take his time. He had to help her discover whatever she needed to discover.

"Come on," he said, forcing his thoughts away from the delicious view of her skin, her wet lips, and her wide blue eyes. He moved past her, hoping that pushing her out of his line of vision would help him collect some strength.

But he could still smell her.

And sense her.

And hear her.

His heart hammered and his blood raced and lust raged through him. Instead of grabbing her and pressing her against the wall in a fit of passion, he said, "We'd better get to work on your formula. Time is wasting."

The command seemed to jar her into action. She followed him into the elevator. They stood too close to each other for comfort, but then there wasn't much Cain could do about it. They would be very close for the next few days, possibly weeks—until the formula was perfected and he moved into the second phase of his assignment.

He drew in another breath and tried to focus on the rising elevator rather than his rising body temperature. With any luck, they would make a major discovery tonight—because he wasn't sure if he could keep from touching her. And touching her, seducing her, wasn't part of the plan.

Not yet.

It is him.

Sophie tried to digest the truth. She was standing next to the man who'd starred in her wild dream last night. A man she'd never seen before, but who made her ache with an impossible desire.

Was he just a man?

Memories of last night rushed in on her, from the Devil's appearance to the dream with this man.

"Who exactly are you?" she asked.

"I thought we already established that. My name is Cain."

"Are you—"

"Merely a helper," he explained. He cast her a glance, his green eyes transfixing her for a long, breathless moment. "But I can see why you wonder. My master does like to shape-shift. I once saw him look exactly like Colonel Sanders. And Benji."

"Benji?"

"The dog. He does canines extremely well. And snakes, but then that should be obvious considering his history."

They lapsed into a moment of silence while Sophie's mind raced. She tried to absorb what she was hearing. Last night had, indeed, been real. She'd called the Devil, and now she was talking to one of his helpers. Forget desperate. She'd gone off the deep-end. Crazy with a capital C. The Devil didn't exist. Nothing existed. Nothing on such a grand scale, at least.

She didn't realize she'd spoken out loud until she heard the man's voice.

"You don't really believe that, or you wouldn't have called him in the first place." Cain's voice grew deeper, huskies. "You believe in good and evil, Sophie. Light and dark. Life and death." His gaze drilled into hers for several frantic heartbeats before he turned to stare up at the flashing numbers of the descending elevator.

"In the deepest part of you, you believe—and that's why I'm here."

She believed, all right.

She believed in Death. But not for Kara. The little girl's image pushed into her head and gave Sophie focus. She blew out a deep breath and struggled for another. "So you work for the Devil? Like an assistant or something?"

"I'm a demon."

Her gaze traveled the length of his body, from his long blond hair pulled back into a neat ponytail at the nape of his neck, to the soft white cotton of his T-shirt that tucked into the waist of his faded blue jeans. Black leather biker boots completed his outfit. A day's growth of stubble covered the lean line of his jaw. Rippling biceps stretched the arms of his T-shirt. Muscles bulged beneath the thin material of his jeans as he moved torward her.

Sophie's breath caught as the elevator stopped. She watched Cain exit and head down the hall toward her laboratory.

He was tall and sexy and handsome.

Too tall.

Too sexy.

Too handsome. She chased after him.

"You don't look like a demon," she said as she caught up.

"Really?" He spared her a quick glance, his brow arched. "Do you speak from experience?"

"No. Yes. I mean, I haven't actually seen one,

95

but I know what they're supposed to look like."

"Don't tell me. Big horns, red eyes and lizard-like tongues."

"No. That's forked tongues and lizard-like skin."

A hint of a grin appeared at the corner of his mouth, and the effect sent a wash of heat through Sophie's body. "I stand corrected." His gaze locked with hers and for a split second she saw a spark in the sea-green depths, like sunlight reflecting off a deep ocean.

"And tails. They have tails," she rambled. At least, nearly every picture she'd ever seen of demons depicted tails.

"You're talking about Beelzebub. He has a tail and horns and red eyes and even lizard-like skin, but he's the exception. He's one of the original spirits of evil reserved solely for nightmares." He waved his hands next to his face as if he was trying to scare her, but then he said. "I'm not here to frighten you though, Sophie." His gaze lingered on hers and her stomach jumped. Not with fear, but with excitement.

He was going to help her save Gwen's child. That was why her heart jumped and lurched forward like a runaway train.

That was the *only* reason.

"A demon is a spirit," he went on, "and a spirit is merely the shadow of one's previous self. Had I been a red-eyed, lizard-looking creature when I lived and breathed, I would resemble one now.

I wasn't. I was once a man, and therefore my spirit mimics its original form."

She couldn't help herself; she reached out and touched his arm. Hair-dusted skin tickled her fingertips. He was hard and warm and *real*.

A knowing smile curved his lips. As if he read her thoughts he said, "I am real, sweet Sophie. And 'tis almost the Witching Hour. I will grow even warmer, even more real as the clock ticks toward midnight. At that time it will be impossible to see me as anything but a man. My energy will be at its peak." He shrugged and turned away. "As morning approaches, however, as the night gives way to daylight, I will lose my strength and grow weak. By the crack of dawn, what you see will fade. I will be but a true shadow during the day."

"You're a ghost."

He turned back and shook his head. "Not exactly. A ghost is a spirit of the dead that refuses to cross over to the other side. I have already crossed over." A strange light glittered in his eyes. "I am paying the price for mistakes. A ghost, completely different, doesn't want to believe they are actually dead. They refuse to see the truth and so they are stuck in the human world, but aren't human. They're not quite dead." His gaze locked with hers. "But I suppose it's the same premise. A spirit is energy. Ghosts are more visible at night, just as I am. They would be able to communicate. To walk and talk and mimic the people that they were. And for both ghosts and demons, during the day the spirit must rest and rejuvenate."

"That's why you disappeared this morning."

"Yes. I had to wait for evening to come to you."

"I told myself that last night was just a dream."

"No. 'Twas real. I am real. For now." He glanced at the clock on the far wall before turning his attention to her work. "We should get started."

"Of course." Sophie rushed to her work station, ignoring her usual habit of donning a lab jacket, and reached for her laptop. Unfortunately, in her rush, the edge of her blouse brushed the small blue flame flickering beneath a test beaker. The material caught. As fire flared up, pain bolted through her.

Crying out, she slapped at the flaming fabric. A heartbeat later, a large hand closed over the flame snuffing it like a candle damper.

"You should be more careful," Cain said. Pulling back the charred material, he examined her.

"It's a hazard of the job," she blurted, then sucked in a breath of air as his fingertips trailed over the small patch of her angry burnt skin. "I keep a first-aid kit in one of the cabinets over there." She indicated the far wall made up of dozens of cabinets, then pulled away from his grasp. "You might want to use a little burn spray, too."

"What for?"

"You put out that flame with your hand. If I'm burned, you have to be—" The words stalled as she stared at his palm and saw only smooth flesh.

Correction: she saw *energy*. This wasn't flesh and blood, regardless how warm or strong or human Cain felt. This was a being made of energy, a shadow that gained substance once darkness fell, no sunlight sapped his strength.

This was a demon.

A million thoughts rushed through her head as she inhaled a deep breath. "I . . ." She started to trail her fingertips over his palm, but Cain balled his fingers and pulled away.

"I'm fine."

"Then, could you grab the kit for me?" She needed a distraction from him. Better yet, he needed a distraction from her—something to look at, to study, besides her. With his attention turned to something else, she might actually breathe.

He examined her arm once more, a frown on his face, before he nodded and turned.

"It's that one over there—" she began, but he'd already zeroed in on the cabinet. A few seconds later, he'd retrieved the kit and handed it to her.

"How did you know which cabinet?" Before

he could answer, she shook her head. "Don't tell me. You saw through the door like Superman."

"Superman?"

"The comic-book hero." She shook her head. "You saw it with some special ability?"

He looked amused. "Do you mean my 'sight'? No. I must actually touch something for that to kick in. Then I'd see impressions of that specific object, impressions from the future. I only knew the whereabouts of the kit because you looked in that direction and I noticed your gaze."

He took the ointment from her trembling hand and applied it to her burn. She winced.

"Does it hurt so much?"

"I'll live. Thankfully, I had the flame on low or it might have been much worse." She looked at him wryly. "I can only imagine what hell must be like."

Suddenly, she couldn't say why, but the minute the words were out, the reality of what she'd done hit her.

Fire.

Brimstone.

Hell.

For the first time, the reality of her bargain last night terrified her. She'd made a deal with the Devil. She'd sold her *soul*.

Fire.

Brimstone.

Hell.

For *eternity*.

Fear swamped her as she put a small bandage over her burn and taped the edges. Her hands trembled and her lips quivered, and she did the only thing she could at that moment: She turned her attention to her laptop.

"We need to hurry this up," she said. "We've got work to do." She keyed in her security code. The screen flickered and she accessed her private-notes file. With a few clicks, she entered a new page. "Okay, shoot."

Cain didn't say anything. Instead, he picked up a vial of blue liquid and sniffed.

"That's liquid nitrogen, calcium sulfite and crystal sulfur."

He nodded and picked up a petrie dish that contained a sand-colored powder. After a sniff, he dipped the tip of his finger into the compound and tested its texture. "And this?"

"That's clam shell ground into a fine powder. It's used in some of our cleansers, but the protein also makes a good moisturizer. It replenishes the skin's elasticity. There's also a small amount of calcium that feeds individual cells and promotes reproduction. Is that part of the right formula?"

"Maybe." He nodded and picked up another dish.

"Maybe?"

"Probably." He sniffed a third dish, then set it to the side and reached for a fourth.

"I didn't promise my soul for 'probably.' I need a concrete answer. Just tell me."

"It doesn't work that way. There are rules for everything in the universe."

"What are you talking about?"

"There's a reason that the Evil One had to send me. He couldn't simply give you the answer to your question because he doesn't know the answer."

"How can that be? He's the Devil. He can read my thoughts and change shapes and appear out of nowhere just like that." She snapped her fingers.

"The sun seems all-powerful during the high heat of noon, but when the day is done, the earth gives way to darkness. That darkness gives way to the dawn. While the Evil One has power, he isn't all-powerful. If he were, darkness would be eternal and there would be no light."

"You're saying there's a cosmic scale."

"Sort of. The Evil One knows many things. He knows all that has happened in the past, and he learns what is happening in the present as it happens. He knows your thoughts, your dreams, and your desires, but he can't know that which does not yet exist. You haven't made this discovery yet."

"How can he bargain with me then? If he can't deliver, then he's of no use."

"Ah, but he *can* deliver. He sent me to help

you in your quest. I can help you make the discovery, one you likely won't make without me. At least, not anytime soon."

"How do you know that if you don't know the future?"

"I don't *know* it, but I can see the enormity of what you're facing. Thousands of trials await you. There's not enough time in the day. Of course, you might always get lucky. There's always a chance."

"A slim one."

Cain looked at her and his eyes blazed. "Which is why I'm here to help. I *can* help, but it will take time for me to familiarize myself with all of this, to get a feel for it. To *feel* it."

"I don't understand."

"That's what I do," he explained. "Or rather, what I did long ago when I was a man. I have a special gift. A sixth sense. Some might refer to it as ESP, precognition. When I concentrate on something, be it an object or person, I start to get impressions. Images. Glimpses into the future."

"You're psychic."

"Psychic, mystic, a witch—I've been called many things. I have the 'sight.' That's all I know for sure, and it will show me when the formula is right—without a series of trials. The gift is even stronger now because as a spirit, my senses are heightened. I will watch you in your experiments, guide you, and ultimately give you the answer. If you still want it. Do you? Do you want my help? Enough to trade your soul?"

Sophie turned away. "You're right. Time's a-wasting." She punched a button on her computer. The screen flickered and her latest notes appeared. The cursor flickered at the last experiment where she'd left off.

Cain touched her shoulder. "You haven't answered my question. Do you want my help enough to trade your soul to my master?"

She meant to say the words, to give in, but the only thing that came out was, "I haven't called security to have you escorted out, have I?"

"That's not good enough, dear Sophie." In the blink of an eye, Cain was beside her, surrounding her with his warmth, his scent, his strength. His arms came up on either side of her, his long fingers splayed on the table top, his arms anchoring her. Hard muscle brushed against her. His stubble-roughened jaw brushed the shell of her ear and a shiver rippled through her.

His voice, low and deep and husky, echoed through her head. "You have to say the words. Unless you've changed your mind." He was so close that she could feel the vibration of his mouth with every word. Yet he didn't actually touch her. "Have you?"

Yes. The word screamed through her thoughts, spurred by the knot of fear formed in her stomach the moment she'd felt Hell's flames in the burning mark on her arm. There would be more flames should she continue on this path. More pain. An eternity's worth.

Yet a lifetime of health, a chance at true happiness for Kara. The daughter of her friend would have a chance. That thought helped her swallow the lump in her throat.

"I want your help."

"How much?"

"Enough to trade my soul."

His next words surprised her: "You don't have to." His voice drew her around to face him, and if she hadn't already seen for herself exactly who he was, *what* he was—if she didn't know for certain he was the Dark One's minion—she might have thought she saw regret in the dark depths of his eyes. "You can turn me away right now and forget the deal. You were misled. You said so yourself. My master doesn't have the answer you seek; he has only agreed to let me help you. Now that you know the truth, it brings the agreement into a different light. You can still turn away, sweet Sophie, and save yourself."

She found herself blushing. He was here to make good on the deal, not to talk her out of it. Wasn't he? Yet here he was giving her an out. A choice.

But she had no choice. She could only do what she was doing.

No choice.

No chance.

No other hope.

She blinked against a sudden blur of tears. "Enough to gladly trade my soul," she repeated. Wiping her eyes, she caught a tear before it could break free. "Can we please get started?"

Cain reached for another petrie dish with a different compound. "The lady has spoken."

It doesn't work. It's breaking apart.

Disappointment rushed through Sophie for the tenth time that evening as she observed the latest failure beneath her microscope.

She slid a new sample of skin beneath its lens. Adding a dropper of another freshly mixed compound, she followed by adding several drops of a different solution that promoted cell erosion. Several seconds ticked by with nothing happening.

Then, slowly, surely . . . the cells started to retract and wither. And, ultimately, to die.

She sighed, looking at the clock. At least she'd put off the process for a full two and a half minutes. She turned to Cain. "The stabilizer is still not right. We must have the wrong combination. We must be missing an ingredient. It's just not right."

"You look tired," he said.

Sophie wiped at her eyes and gulped the last of some cold coffee. "I'm fine, or I will be once the next pot finishes brewing." She indicated

106

the small coffeemaker that sat in the far corner. "That's the key."

"You need rest, not more caffeine."

She gave him an annoyed look. "Coffee keeps my eyes open. Sleep doesn't." She checked off the latest failure in her notes and reached for another microscope slide. The ingredients were close by, so she started to mix the next compound on her schedule this time adding a drop of a well-known stabilizing agent.

She knew all the various agents that could be used, so why didn't she just know which would actually do the trick?

Or how much?

Why did it all have to be a matter of trial and error?

Thinking of what she had to do, she tried to gather energy.

More possible combinations.

More experiments.

More time.

She drew in a deep breath and rubbed her eyes.

Cain moved closer to her. "Why don't you stretch out on the sofa over there and take a small break?" His deep voice pushed past the throbbing in her temples. "We've made some progress."

"Some, yes. Enough, no."

"Rome wasn't built in a day, Sophie."

"The Romans must have had more than a day to spare. I don't."

Cain stared at her, his eyes intense. "This is not going to happen tonight. Be content with our progress, and regain your strength."

She should. She was so tired now that she could hardly think. It was nearly five o'clock in the morning. She'd gone nearly twenty-four hours without sleep. Maybe he could continue without her.

"Can you work with the stabilizers for a little while, see if any of them jumps out at you? Touch them and see if you can summon anything."

"Yes. If you rest."

He pointed to the couch. She nodded, then walked over and dropped down onto it. She could take a break. A small break. Five minutes.

Leaning back, she closed her eyes.

Ten minutes max. And only because they had made progress. They'd shortened months of work into six short hours; Cain had eliminated several chains of mixtures without her even having to test them.

The progress eased some of Sophie's anxiety, and she actually smiled. Also, it wasn't as if all work would cease now when she took a few minutes to herself. She had help now. Cain was here with her, helping her.

Yes, love. I'm here. I'm right here.

The voice, so rich and deep, whispered through her head and lulled her muscles to relax. Was she imagining it? Was this what she wanted him to say to her? She felt herself sinking into slumber, but the voice remained.

I'm here helping you.

Watching over you.

Touching you.

In a startling instant, she imagined the heat of a hand, the play of fingertips. Oh, what a dream this was! And as much as she wanted to pull away—to stop herself from focusing on anything but her work—she found herself sinking more fully into the dream. Because as much as she wanted undisturbed rest, she suddenly wanted to fantasize about Cain's touch even more.

Chapter Seven

Cain could see heaven, but he couldn't quite touch it: She lay on her back on the small sofa in the far corner of her laboratory. She was in much the same pose as she'd been the night before in her living room.

Her dark hair had come loose from its ponytail. The long, silky strands spilled around her head, a stark contrast against the bland beige upholstery. Her blouse had ridden up just enough to give him a luscious view of her smooth, tanned abdomen.

His gaze lingered on Sophie's belly button, and he had the incredible urge to dip his tongue inside, to swirl it around and taste the salty sweetness of her skin.

Just once.

That's what he told himself, but the beast raged too fiercely within him to be satisfied with such a meager offering. Cain rooted himself to his spot several feet away.

He couldn't touch yet—not with his hands, at least—but he could look.

Summoning magic, he made a small motion with his fingers. Sophie's top button slid free. Then another. And another. The silk of her blouse finally fell open; its front slithered to either side.

Sophie's lips parted as she must have felt the cold sweep of air against her bare flesh. She dragged in a breath and her chest rose, her breasts rising and pushing against the skimpy lace of her no-nonsense white bra. Her nipples were dark shadows beneath that flimsy covering.

Cain blew softly. Sophie's nipples hardened. Both ripe tips peaked up against the lace to tempt him. His mouth watered, and he drew in his own deep breath.

Not that he was actually breathing. He was energy that only mimicked a man's form, a man's physical responses. His chest rose and fell as if drinking in precious oxygen, but it was all just an illusion. He was not alive anymore. For many reasons, the thought saddened him. Tension held him, though, every fiber of his being stretched as taut as a newly strung guitar. Pressure pulsed in his groin as he felt himself harden. He sensed his pulse rose—as if blood still flowed and primed him the way it had so very long ago!

He *was* a man. Or at least he responded as one, looked like one at that this moment. Now, when night was at its darkest, the veils between the worlds its thinnest, undoubtedly she would see a man were she to open her eyes. She would feel a man were she to reach out.

The thought sent a wave of heat through him, his nerves screaming, the hunger raging the way it always did. Yet there was something different this time. He felt this attraction to Sophie Alexander more fiercely than any he'd ever felt before with any other woman in his past.

Why was that? And why had he acted so solicitous of her health? He'd never been so tied to a woman before, in life *or* in death. At least, not for a long time.

As a mortal he'd had many women, all leading up to and paling in comparison to one—his first true love. His last true love. He'd never loved again.

Of course he'd never abstained from sex. Women had been his for the taking even before he'd become an incubus. He'd never fought back his desire. The urge to have this woman, to sate his lust on her, was a familiar one. Lust he understood; the other emotions were what he was having trouble with. The surges of protectiveness that filled him. The rushes of compassion. The desire to simply feel Sophie's skin, to see if it felt as soft as it looked, as smooth, as delicate.

Deprivation. That's what it is.

Sex deprivation was what was causing such crazy thoughts. He'd never had to deal with this abstinance before. Always before his only objective was to seduce women and find release. The quicker the better.

By Odin, I'm an incubus!

"An incubus with a special talent that I must use right now." The Evil One's words echoed in Cain's head and Cain's fingers bunched into fists. *"I want that formula, but in order to get it, you must help her find it. Find it, Cain. Find it, or suffer my anger instead of my joy. I've seen your compassion for this woman. It confuses me. And you touched her during that first meeting although I expressly forbade it. Did I not tell you to stick to dreams? I do not want her waking hours in any way distracted."*

An icy coldness slithered around Cain, a giant serpent working its way up his body until he found himself completely immobile. The restraint tightened, squeezing the very essence out of him, warning him of the pain and suffering to come should he fail in this task.

The pressure grew more intense, consuming, until he could hear nothing, feel nothing, see nothing except darkness. In that instant, he knew what true Hell would be like. He'd been spared it until now. There would be no lingering in this world, no losing himself in the heat of a warm body and forgetting everything for several brief blissful moments. There would be nothing but the bizarre half-state he endured while the sun rode high in the sky and chased away the shadows. Except there would be pain, too. Already day by day he endured that oblivion, with only the coming night to provide any reprieve. He could tell himself the visions that haunted him there would vanish with twilight.

But if he failed? There would only be an eternity to remember the past, to dwell on it, to regret it. And all while suffering physical torment.

"Find the answer and you will move on to another assignment. Another sweet, warm woman. Another distraction," came the Evil One's voice.

" 'Tis my punishment," Cain agreed.

"Yes. One you willingly embrace—which makes it little punishment at all. Cain, true punishment would be dwelling in the darkness forever, with nothing but your conscience for company. And I can also throw in the traditional fire and brimstone: the flames licking at you, burning and consuming, forever and ever. Is that what you want? Would you really trade your place at my side for that? Give up any hope of doing anything but my will, won't you, Cain?"

Through the haze of pain, he managed to nod.

"I thought so. Act swiftly, Cain. Do my bidding.

Otherwise you will know what punishment truly is."

The coldness eased and in its place Cain felt heat—a raging heat that surrounded him. Flames licked at his body, burned and ravaged and his every nerve screamed with pain. Cain twisted and writhed, but there was no escape.

Then, as quickly as it had come, the fire died, doused by a great wind that smelled of death and darkness. The blackness lifted and Cain found himself back in the laboratory. He glanced down at his arms where the fire had burned hottest, but there was nothing but rough, hair-dusted skin and the memory of unbearable agony.

His gaze shifted to the woman on the couch. It was all he could do to keep his distance, but he would, for even more than his strange desire for her, he feared the fire and darkness.

She breathed deeply, her chest lifting, and he felt the lust roar inside him. But it was deep inside him, where it would stay.

But the Evil One had said he could continue to watch her, to feed her dreams. In the end, she would want him so much that she would do whatever he wanted. She would even hand over their formula for one night in his arms. His master had been right to insist on this course of action.

One night. Thinking about it made him ache. One night was all he needed from her—all Cain the Slayer needed from any one woman. A few hours of sweet, blissful surrender, and then he could move on.

But first would be a wait.

He was touching her.

There was no mistaking the sure stroke of his warm fingertips that trailed from her toes and traced the slope of her foot, the curve of her ankle, the length of her calf. She moaned but kept her eyes closed. She would not acknowledge this.

Lazy circles teased the inside of one knee, pleasantly melting bone and muscle, until she parted her legs for him. Open and trembling, she waited while he stroked upward, inch by slow, tantalizing inch.

"Do you like that?"

Cain's deep voice pushed past the roar of her own heartbeat and slid into Sophie's ears, seducing her senses much the way his touches seduced her body.

"Do you?" he repeated.

She nodded, her breath coming too fast to accommodate anything more than a faint whimper.

"You do, don't you?" he accused. His touch slid back down toward her knee. He traced more circles, so slow and sinfully light that she wanted to cry. It had been so long since a man had touched her like this.

The warmth of his hand slid up again, skimming the tender inside of her thigh. She gasped.

Actually, no man had ever touched her in quite this way, despite her vast experience. A bad girl—and she'd been bad since the moment she'd realized a call from an irate teacher caught her parents' attention much more than a straight-A report card—always had experience. Hers had started back in her hometown of Houston during her freshman year at Sharpstown High. The senior captain of the football team had sought her out to tutor him in chemistry. He'd smiled and she'd smiled, and the bargain had been struck. She'd lent him her scientific expertise, and he'd schooled her in the art of sex.

He'd only been seventeen, his experience limited to the back seat of his souped-up Chevy Impala, and so her first time hadn't been that great. But the mussed-up hair and the coming home late had earned more attention from her parents in one, lecture-filled evening than she'd seen in an entire year.

She'd had many lovers after. At first, the shock value had motivated her to seek them out. To kiss and pet and build a reputation that would aggravate her conservative, workaholic parents and gain their attention—if only for a lengthy lecture session or a week's worth of grounding.

Later, as she turned from a rebellious girl into

117

a headstrong woman, she sought members of the opposite sex for more than an act of anger against her family. She'd sought them out for her own pleasure.

Yet none—not even her steady back in college with whom she'd had her longest relationship to date: two years—had ever stirred sensation like this.

She moaned again.

He moved higher. Closer.

"I . . ." She sucked in a sharp breath as his fingertips grazed the elastic edge of her panties. Her body throbbed and she felt the moisture gather between her legs. She whimpered.

"*I know you do.*" A few lazy circles and she moaned. "*You like it and you want more. Don't you?*"

She nodded slightly and he made a *tsk-tsk* sound.

"*That's not good enough, girl. I must hear the words. Tell me you want more, Sophie. You've got to tell me.*"

One fingertip stroked across the crotch of her panties, up and down, tracing the soft flesh beneath.

"*Say the words.*"

As if she could say anything! She was too fraught with desire.

And also, if she were completely honest, deep down inside a part of her didn't want to. She wanted to stay focused on her project, and somehow knew that admitting this need gripping her from the inside out would be a mistake. It would be a complication. Another worry when she already had all the worries she could take.

Focus.

She tried to open her eyes, to work past the passionate haze overpowering her senses. She turned her head toward the lights blazing at her work station, tried to hear the whir of the air conditioner or the hum of her computer—anything save the thundering of her heart and the soft panting that vibrated her lips. But she couldn't even open her eyes. She could only feel.

The rush of heat through her body, the electricity zipping up and down her spine, the fingertip moving up and down, side to side . . .

"Oh!" she gasped.

His finger had slipped under the elastic band of her panties and slicked along her bare flesh. The moan had worked its way up her throat involuntarily. Heat swelled from the point of his contact, rising through Sophie's body like hot lava bubbling to the surface of a volcano.

Higher, higher.

Hotter, hotter.

She squirmed, trying to draw his finger inside. He moved it closer to the point of entry, and she arched. Just a little more and he would be in, filling her up, taking away the loneliness and isolation that had plagued her for most of her life.

What?

"You like that and you want more." His words weren't a question this time, but a statement. He didn't ask her to say anything, but she knew, in order to feel him, to really feel him, she would have to voice her need.

To ask.

To beg.

She was desperate to, but something held her back. Something that told her to focus. To think.

"You can't resist me, Sophie. You want me too much and you have a right. You're a beautiful woman. Desirable. You deserve more than this laboratory, more than an empty apartment with no one to come home to. No one to peel off your clothes and thrust inside and take your mind off all your problems. No one to rub your feet and kiss your nipples and tell you all of the things you want so desperately to hear. Things every woman has a right to hear. That you're beautiful. Vivacious. Sexy. Desirable. You don't have anyone right now. You're alone. Lonely."

The word stirred the desperation inside her and summoned a picture of Kara. While her relationship with her goddaughter was far removed from what he was talking about—a passionate bond between a man and a woman— it still filled a crucial void in her life.

She wasn't lonely.

Not now.

Not yet.

Not if she stayed focused on the task at hand.

"You don't have to be lonely anymore."

"I'm not," she breathed, fighting to regain her composure against the onslaught of sensation. "I won't be—" Her words faded into a shrill sound that shattered the haze surrounding her.

Her eyes snapped open and she stared up to see . . .

A ceiling dotted with shafts of light peeking past the nearby blinds.

No man looming over her, long thick hair the color of summer wheat framing his chiseled face and high cheekbones and sculpted nose. No sensuous mouth slanted at the corners in a seductive grin that said he knew all of her deepest, most erotic desires.

Because he was her deepest, most erotic desire and now he had a face and a name.

Cain.

Her gaze darted around the room, but there was no one there. Just empty corners and a fierce quiet that told her she'd been dreaming.

Dawn peeked past the edges of the lowered blinds and in a startling instant she realized that it was morning. A glance at the clock confirmed it. Ten A.M.

She'd slept half the night away.

Or rather, she'd dreamt it away.

She glanced down and noted her slacks were still zipped, her shirt still buttoned. The edges of her silk blouse hung loose, but that was undoubtedly from tossing and turning while she slept. Otherwise, nothing was amiss. Not like last night when she'd done more than just fantasize.

She'd touched and stroked and . . .

She drew in a shaky breath and stared at her workstation. While the seduction had been a dream, Cain was all too real.

The proof stared back at her from the lab station where she'd been working the night before. Sophie's gaze zeroed in on the test beaker that bubbled with the blue compound base they'd mixed and tested last night: a stabilizing compound that had actually prevented cell deterioration for a full two and a half minutes.

There'd been no merely slowing it down. They'd actually managed to stop it for longer than the thirty seconds afforded by the active ingredient.

While thirty seconds was nothing, it was a step in the right direction. Thirty seconds meant they were on the right track. One step closer to an answer.

A perfected stabilizer would maintain the mixture in its active state for even longer. Days. Weeks. Months. Maybe even years.

Yeah, right.

The fear inside her refused to let her truly believe in something quite so extraordinary. But she didn't have to have a one shot compound that preserved cell stasis for an indefinite amount of time. All she had to do was sustain the results for a week, if possible, maybe even a few days longer. A reasonable length of time that would lend itself to an effective treatment plan.

It wasn't within reason to expect the formula to be administered every hour or so. No one could lead a good quality of life with such a burden. But a week? A month? While the month would be preferable, a weekly treatment plan would be doable.

Something within reason, such as four doses per month to prevent any more cells falling victim to disease, be it deterioration or leukemia.

A shrill sound exploded in the quiet, the same sound that had pierced her thoughts. Her cell phone.

She pushed from the couch, tucking in her blouse as she headed toward her desk and retrieved her phone.

One glance at the display and she realized she wasn't getting a phone call, but a digital page.

911.

Her heart turned over and her stomach hollowed out. Frantically, she punched the buttons, dialed her apartment and listened as the phone rang.

123

One . . . two . . .

"Come on," she muttered as she snatched up her purse and rushed toward the door. There was only one person who would send such a page. Beth. It meant something was wrong with Kara.

"Please pick up." But there was no one there to hear her plea. Only the continual ringing.

Nine . . . ten . . . eleven . . .

Out in the hall, she punched in the security code for her laboratory. Nothing happened. Another frantic punch and the red light still flashed. "What the heck—"

"It's the new security codes." The comment came from Jana Smith, one of the laboratory assistants who worked in product enhancement across the hall. She held a steaming cup of coffee in one hand and a bagel in the other. "It took me fifteen minutes to open my door this morning." She turned her attention to punching the display that sat next to her door. "Crazy, that's what all this James Bond bull is. Espionage? More like a paranoid woman who can't admit when someone gets the jump on her."

Sophie turned back to her own display and closed her eyes, trying to remember. A few punches and . . . there. It was green. She rushed for the elevator and pushed her way into the crowd when the doors swung open.

"Hi, Sophie."

"Hey, Miss Alexander."

"What's up?"

The greetings echoed around her, but Sophie could do little more than nod. Her full attention focused on the cell phone in her hands and the ring that echoed in her ears.

Thirteen . . . fourteen . . . fifteen . . .

The elevator doors swished open and she hit the hallway at a near run as she headed for the parking garage.

Nineteen . . . twenty . . . twenty-one . . .

It was no use. She punched the OFF button on the phone as she climbed into the car. Keying the engine, she shoved the gear into reverse and hit the gas.

There was no answer.

No comforting voice at the other end to assure her that everything was all right. That Kara was still well, still in remission, still alive.

Nothing but an emergency page still blinking on the phone's digital display, and the terrible feeling that Sophie's worst fear had finally come true.

"Happy Birthday!"

The words rang out the minute Sophie shoved open the door to her darkened apartment. The lights flicked on, the shades lifted, and she saw a smiling Kara standing in the middle of the living room. She wore her favorite

Barbie shirt, matching shorts, a Barbie party hat and pink frosting on her nose.

Even more, she was alive and breathing, her color good, her eyes lit with excitement rather than fear.

Relief washed through Sophie and she wanted to laugh and cry at the same time. Instead, she dropped her briefcase at the door, crossed the room and dropped to her knees. She wiped the smudge from the girl's nose and relished the feel of warm, soft flesh. "You've got frosting on your face."

"I tried to keep her out of the cake," Beth said, coming up behind Kara. "But you know how much she loves sweets."

Kara turned an accusing gaze on Sophie. "You took too long. 911 means emergency. It means to come home right away."

"Speaking of which, I was worried sick, little girl."

"I'm so sorry," Beth said, pulling off her own party hat. "I didn't want to let her do that, but you said you would be home for breakfast and when you didn't show, she was upset."

"Breakfast is at seven A.M. It's after *ten*," Kara said. "Beth missed her first class and everything."

"It's no big deal. It was Greek theology in the tenth century. I hate Greeks. Jack, my ex boyfriend was Greek."

"Thirty minutes after," Kara added.

"I tried calling the lab earlier," Beth told her, "but your phone calls were going to voice mail just like your cell phone. That's when Kara said to 911 you and, well, you do usually respond to a page like that pretty quick."

"I tried to call a little while ago."

"I'm not a good liar and I knew you would want to know what was up, so I didn't answer."

"What if I had answered at the lab?"

"I was going to lie. I would have had to have lied, but this way I had an option."

"One that worried me sick."

"Sorry," Beth said again before shooting Kara an I-told-you-so look.

"*You* had *me* worried sick," Kara said. "You were s'posed to be home at seven."

"I worked late and fell asleep on the couch."

"But you're home now and it's time for your surprise party." She pulled a pink box from behind her. "Ta-da."

"You got me a present?"

"We can't have a surprise party without presents," Kara informed her. She shoved the small box with the large pink bow into Sophie's hands. "This is mine. Open it first."

Sophie settled herself on the couch and let Kara slip the party hat on her head before she turned her attention to the present.

A few seconds later, she pulled back the tissue paper to stare down at a child's drawing that had been matted and framed.

"That's us," Kara told her as she pointed to two stick figures holding hands. A bright yellow smiley-faced sunshine stared down at the two figures surrounded by various colored flowers. "That's our garden that we're going to have when I don't have to see the doctors anymore and we can move away from here. There's poppies and carnations and violets. I'd like some roses, too, but I don't like all those thorns. Do they have roses without thorns?"

Sophie blinked back a sudden surge of tears. "I don't really know."

"We should find out. We can have daisies, too, can't we?"

She smiled. "We can have anything you want, sweetie."

"No we can't." Kara gave her a frown. "Don't say that."

"Why not?"

"Because you only say that when I'm sick and I'm not sick anymore."

"No, you're not." It was true. Right now, at this moment, she wasn't sick, and Sophie was one step closer to seeing that she stayed that way.

"There's our pig," Kara pointed to a small pink figure in one corner. "And here's his sister." She pointed to another. "And his brother. And his aunt. And his cousin." Her gaze shifted to Sophie. "If you had kids, would they be my cousins?"

"Only if I was your aunt. I'm not."

"I wish you were."

"I'm something better. I'm your godmother. That means that I'm the next best thing to a mommy if yours can't be here."

"So if you had kids they would be my brothers and sisters?"

She nodded.

"I think I want a brother. And a sister. And a pig."

"You're not giving up on the pig, are you?"

"Two pigs, remember? So that the other doesn't get lonely."

"Two pigs," Sophie agreed. "Speaking of which, I think I could use a big piece of cake."

"Two pieces," Kara chimed in. "I'm really hungry."

Sophie smiled. "Me, too."

"Count me in," Beth added. "I'm officially solo. Chocolate cake with pink frosting is the closest thing to ecstasy I'll get for some time."

"What's x-tasty?" Kara asked.

"Nothing," Sophie and Beth said in unison. "Let's eat.

129

Chapter Eight

Cain watched her as she moved about the laboratory and prepared for the night's experiments.

Night.

That's all he awaited. For the sun to set, the shadows to take over and his strength to completely renew itself.

It was close.

Outside the high-rise windows, the sun crept below the horizon. The night lights had already switched on outside, the street lamps blazing. Only a desk lamp blazed in the laboratory. Shadows crouched in the corners, providing the portal he'd needed to leave behind the nothingness and his damned thoughts, and step into the real world.

Still, it was early and he wasn't his full self. Certainly she could see him right now if he wanted her to. He wasn't so weak as to be transparent. But he didn't want her to see him.

He liked blending into the background, watching her, studying her without her seeing his interest.

A curiosity that had nothing to do with lust and everything to do with the way she wrinkled her brow while she loaded the slides beneath her microscope, as if the one act required all of her attention when she'd undoubtedly done it time and time again. She had such determination.

Then, of course, there was the way her nose crinkled and her eyes lit up when she retrieved the framed picture from her briefcase. A child's drawing depicting flowers and pink pigs.

His attention shifted to several similar drawings attached to a nearby file cabinet with various magnets. More flowers and pink pigs and lots of sunshine.

He'd noticed the illustrations the night before, but he hadn't given them much thought. Not with Sophie so close to him, stirring his senses like no other. She affected him more fervently than the endless number of women in his past. He'd come to terms with the intensity of his reaction while waiting on the other side for night to fall, and he'd concluded that she was different because the situation was different.

He was stuck in a strictly hands-off situation. No touching, so it was only natural that he would want to touch.

That had been the way of things since the beginning of time. The forbidden always attracted the most attention and stirred the most desire. Man had always wanted what he could not have, and Cain, while more than a man now, was still no exception.

In fact, he wanted more fiercely.

He ignored the burst of heat that the one thought stirred and turned his attention back to Sophie. He watched as she made room for the picture on the desk in a spot near her computer. Her hands lingered on the frame and her smile faded as she touched one flower and traced it with her fingertip.

Her shoulders trembled. A motion so slight hat it wouldn't have been noticeable to the naked eye, but Cain noticed. He noticed everything about her.

The sudden brightness of her eyes.

The slight quiver of her bottom lip.

His hands tightened and it was all he could do not to cross the room and draw her into his arms and simply hold her and chase away whatever thoughts haunted her. He wanted to feel the pain slip away and her body relax against him.

He wanted to see her smile.

Odin's fist, I'm insane!

Was he so deranged by the past twenty-four hours of abstinance that he'd started to crave the little things, like a hungry dog eager for scraps. A glance. A kind word. A soft expression.

By all that was sacred, no! He wanted her complete surrender.

He shifted his attention away from her and studied her laboratory. He'd been so busy, so anxious and needy the night before that it had taken every molecule of his energy to focus on the various chemical compounds. There'd been no chance to take in his surroundings.

Until now.

The small office carved into one corner of the massive room stood out in complete contrast to the clinical white of the lab. There was a leopard-print chair, an oversized pair of shel-lacked cowboy boots that served as paper weights. A large, splatter print hung just above the desk. A James Dean picture graced the wall a few inches away.

For all of her professionalism when it came to her experiments, she was a rebel at heart. A passionate woman who painted her walls cherry red despite the copies of *Science Today* scattered across her coffee table. A wild child barely contained by her surroundings.

Child. The thought drew his attention back to the picture and he remembered Sophie's words the night before.

I have to help my goddaughter.

Had her goddaughter made the pictures for her?

It made sense, but Cain had no way of being certain.

He knew everything when it came to the feelings of his subjects. He could look at them and know what they were feeling. But he didn't know what caused such emotion. He had to gather that information through conversation and observation.

They'd been too busy to talk last night, and so he watched her now because he'd been unable to the night before. He'd been in such a hurry to get started on the first leg of his mission that he'd failed to note anything except the way she smelled whenever she leaned toward him. The way her face dropped when they failed to uncover all the answers with one simple experiment. The way she'd actually smiled that morning before she'd taken the phone call that had sent her running for the elevator.

He'd wanted to go after her. He'd gone so far as to follow her out the door, but he hadn't made it more than a few feet. Daylight had streamed through the twentieth-floor windows and he'd done as he'd always had to in such a situation—slink back into the shadows. His home for the past thousand years.

His destiny.

He'd been a child of the night the moment

he'd drawn his first breath beneath the light of a full moon. His "sight" had kept him in the shadows because there were those who feared his sixth sense. He'd learned early on, both by experience and by the guidance of his mother, to embrace the darkness.

Close your eyes, my dear son. Don't look. Please, don't look!

His mother's voice whispered through his head the way it had so long ago. A desperate plea by a dying woman who'd wanted her son to remember her alive. But like all children, his curiosity, his fear, had gotten the best of him.

She'd known, and she'd grown even more vehement, determined to spare him.

"Look away, child. Look away," she mouthed with pale lips, her face ashen. Red trickled from the empty cavities where her eyes had once been. They were gone now, trophies to the vicious man who'd taken them, determined to save her from herself. To exorcise the devil that lived and breathed inside her and gave her her sight.

Death hovered so close, surrounding her, sucking the life out, yet she refused to give up until she'd warned her only child one last time. "Please . . ."

But it had been too late.

He'd seen, and that last image had followed him as he'd gone to live with his uncle while his father had hunted the man responsible—an overzealous landlord who'd sought to rid his lands of people he saw as evil. He'd led a campaign against any and all mystics, claiming the tongue of one who conversed with the animals, the hand of one who had the healing touch, the eyes of she who'd seen into the future.

He'd claimed all of their gifts, but he hadn't been any more powerful when it came time to face off with Cain's father. He'd fallen at the first thrust of the sword, but his men had not. They'd overwhelmed Cain's father and slaughtered him, and Cain had been an orphan with only the memory of his precious mother to keep him warm at night.

Warmth?

He'd known no such thing in his childhood. Merely fear. He'd lain awake night after night, afraid that the same man would come for him to claim his eyes, his sight. No one had come, but that had been little comfort. Those who knew about him had regarded him with fear and suspicion, and while no one had lifted a hand, they'd shut him out, made him an outsider.

Over the years, the fear had turned to bitterness. He'd grown into an angry young man who'd stopped praying for acceptance and thrived on his difference. He'd joined a band of warriors and made a name for himself fighting the English. He'd been cunning and ruthless, a rebel with no one and nothing to lose except the anger that kept him warm during those cold, lonely nights. He'd longed for revenge in those days, eager to face his enemy. To face Death and defeat him.

Instead, he'd faced his own mortality and in the process had found something that warmed him even more than vengeance.

Love.

A fool's notion, he'd since realized.

Love made a man weak. It blinded him to the true nature of men and colored his perception of the world. Cain had learned his lesson the hard way. He'd been blind to the danger, optimistic that people could forget their fear of him as both a ruthless warrior and a mystic. That people could forgive his transgressions and see him as merely a man as had the fair lady Felice who'd come to his rescue that cold Autumn morning.

She'd seen him for what he was—a wounded man in need of help—and accepted his gift as a part of him, and he'd loved her for it.

Never again.

"Help me, Cain!" The familiar voice called to him, drawing him to the dark, dank belly of the castle. The coldness crept around him and dread reached out with massive hands to slide around his throat and squeeze . . .

Cain shook the vision away the way he always did. It was over and done with. His wife had lost her life because of him, because his enemies had been resilient in their quest for vengeance and she'd been the instrument of that revenge.

Anger had driven them, just as it had driven him most of his adult life. Until Felice. And after Felice.

He'd gone after her murderer, and he'd delivered his own brand of justice with no thought to the consequence. A first for even a man like Cain.

While he'd been a warrior on the battlefield, he'd never set out to slaughter one individual. Death was a by-product of war. Usually massive and unavoidable. Never specific. Never cold or calculated or so damned satisfying.

It had been all three when he'd plunged the blade deep and held the man's life in his hands.

His life and his death.

He'd twisted the blade and chosen the latter with no remorse or regret. At that moment, he'd felt another blade thrust between his shoulder blades, slicing all in its path.

Only as he lay dying next to the man—the nameless relative of someone Cain had killed in one too many battles—had he felt the first pang of conscience. *Too little too late.* Everything had gone black and he'd met his own death, and there'd been no opportunity to say "I'm sorry."

To reflect.

To regret.

He'd faced off with the Evil One soon after.

Cain had blood on his hands. Blood that could never be washed away. Blood that would forever haunt his deepest thoughts and so he crossed over to the darkness rather than the light.

I did not mean to harm ye, boy. Neither ye nor ye lady. I did not think first. I am sorry. By all that is good in the eyes of Odin, I am truly sorry for killing the boy . . .

The man's words still echoed in his head. Cain had had a few moments as he lay dying next to the man, a few moments to say the words that would ease the man's guilt and his own, but he'd hesitated and then it had been too late.

Something stirred deep inside Cain, but he shook it away, concentrating on the sweet smell of the woman that stood so close. Another deep breath and he stopped thinking altogether. He merely felt.

Fire. Hunger. *Need.*

A soft sigh pushed past the sudden drumming of his heart and he turned his full attention to her where she stood at her workstation. She wore a white lab coat over a plain white cotton blouse tucked into black slacks. Only the red boots she'd worn the night before added any color to the outfit and betrayed the passionate nature he'd glimpsed the night before.

He scanned her from head to toe, his gaze lingering on all the delicious spots in between— the exposed shell of her ear where her hair tucked behind, the curve of her neck, the deep vee where her shirt came together and buttoned, the narrow nip of the belt at her waist, the flare of her hips beneath the slacks.

Her clothing did little for her figure, but it didn't matter. Every curve, every dip had branded itself into his mind last night as he'd watched her, stirred her while she'd lain on the couch and he'd whispered in her ear.

Suggestions.

That's all he'd made. He'd simply said a few suggestive words, let his hair trail over a few prime spots of skin, and her own imagination, her own need, had taken things from there.

His pulse jumped and he felt the pain in his groin as he remembered. A feeling that did nothing to compare with the sudden curiosity that gripped him when he noticed the intent look on her face.

She stood across the room measuring out various chemicals, determination carved into her features as she poured one beaker into another, as if the weight of the world rested on the outcome.

Then again, it did, at least for her. It was her future at stake. Her soul. A sacrifice she was all too willing to make.

Why?

He'd never really cared about the particulars of any given seduction. Women came to him for various reasons. Youth, beauty, money, companionship. He usually knew the reasons. He felt them when he connected to a woman's thoughts. But with Sophie, he felt only despair.

Anguish.

Sadness.

All over an experiment that promised perpetual youth.

But she didn't look like a woman overly concerned with her appearance. She wore very little makeup, her hair pulled back in a loose ponytail. A few strands had come loose and she'd shoved them behind one ear. Her clothes were conservative and low-key with the exception of her boots. She didn't give the appearance of a woman who worried over her looks.

A woman desperate to hold on to her fading youth.

She had very few wrinkles. One or two freckles dotted her otherwise flawless complexion. There wasn't an age spot in sight.

Why?

He watched her as she left the lab station and walked back to her desk to pick up a stack of computer printouts. Her gaze seemed to snag on something and she reached to pick up the single sheet of paper that lay on the far corner of the desk.

He studied her face as she read the paper. Her brow furrowed and her lips thinned, and like everything else about her, he couldn't help but wonder . . .

141

Why?

He didn't realize he'd voiced the question out loud until she turned toward him and her gaze collided with his.

Emotion flashed in her eyes, everything from surprise to curiosity to desire. She licked her lips nervously and pushed several strands of hair that had come loose from her ponytail behind one ear.

"I—I didn't realize you were here."

Ah, but she should have. She should have felt nothing but desire in his presence, as he felt nothing but desire. Because her senses were tuned to his just as his were tuned to hers.

She would have, but she was overwhelmed by too many other things. The experiments that lay ahead. The paper that she still held in her hand.

Where his first instinct would have been to make her forget, to push the distractions away until she forgot all but his presence, suddenly he wanted to understand what she was feeling and why.

Even more, he wanted to help.

Crazy. He was an incubus, not a psychiatrist.

Then again, he was here in a far different capacity at the moment, with an objective that involved more than a breath-stealing seduction.

"What's wrong?"

She stared at him a moment more before tearing her gaze away and glancing at the paper in her hands. "Just a memo." She scanned the page again. "Carol's probably being paranoid."

"Carol?"

"She owns the company. She's convinced someone might try to steal my formula."

As if she sensed his questions, she went on, "We were one-upped on a new product last year. Another company came out with something nearly identical a month earlier and she's convinced it was because of theft. That maybe the competing company had someone on the inside spying on us. I don't think so, but then I can't come up with any other explanation for their product."

"Maybe they just had a similar idea."

"An identical idea." She shook her head. "Maybe, but the odds of winning the lottery with a fifty million pot are more likely. It's too coincidental. She's stepped up security, particularly in this department. New locks. New security codes. The memo's a reminder for everyone to be on guard for anything out of the ordinary and to report any strange occurrences or strange people to security as soon as possible."

A grin tugged at her lips and his groin throbbed in response. "I wonder if a visit from one of the Devil's own would qualify as strange."

"I would think so." The urge to reach out and flick his tongue across her bottom lip, trace the slight crook of her lips filled him. He tightened his fists to keep from reaching out and turned his attention to the workstation. A few strides and he surveyed the two test beakers filled with different liquids.

"These are the two compounds from last night that preserved the cell stasis for two and a half minutes. I'm going to try varying the amounts to see if the time increases. If not, we might have to try a third ingredient. Or even a fourth." She shook her head. "Or a fifth."

"Try varying the amounts first." He picked up the petrie dish. Taking a whiff, he closed his eyes, opening his mind to the smell and the feel of the compound, waiting for the senses to form a vision.

Ah, but there was another smell that kept wafting through his nostrils and stirring a much different vision. One of arms and legs tangled, bodies touching and sliding . . .

"Do you see anything?"

He did. He saw her as she'd been last night. Nearly naked. Panting. *Wanting.*

He shook his head.

"Then I might as well forget this."

"Not yet."

"Then you are seeing something."

"Nothing visual. Just a feel."

"Good, bad?"

"Maybe."

"Maybe to which one? Is it good? Or bad?"

He held the combination to his nose and tried

to focus on the blackness, looking for an opening. A pinpoint of light that would clue him in as to the combination's future. Another sniff and a dot appeared, growing larger, larger. He saw her then as she stood in the lab, a smile on her face as she stared into the microscope.

"There is no third ingredient. Or fourth. It's these two."

Hope flared in her vivid green eyes, only to die a quick death as she stared at the test strip she'd just dipped into the compound. "It's not the right balance. Too much iron. It'll overwhelm the cell tissue and break it down. This can't be it."

She reached for another petrie dish, dipped a dropped into one beaker and deposited a few drops. Repeating the process with the second beaker, she added one drop less. "Those were equal amounts. Let's try this." Another test strip and she frowned. "This isn't it. There's not enough iron and it appears as if there's a small bit of acid producing as a by-product. We need to balance the acid." She reached for another dish filled with a silver powder. "Let's add—"

Her words died as his hand closed over hers. The contact was mesmerizing, like a warm compress pressed up against a frigid forehead. The heat seeped into her, spreading and stirring.

"It's these two compounds. You must work with only these."

145

Doubt glimmered in her eyes. "How can you be so sure?"

He let go of her hand to pull back the sleeve of his shirt. His fingertips touched the familiar scar that marred one bicep. He could still feel the heat as the brand had melted into him, still smell the stench of burning flesh.

"The men who came to murder my mother marked me as her son. They wanted everyone to know who I was. What I was. A mystic. Such was her curse and mine. She was much better at using her gift, however. She saw the future more clearly and so her revelations were often frightening. Too much so for the people in our village who wanted her death. They spared my life that day, but took away my spirit."

"They branded you," she said with disbelief. "Someone actually *branded* you." She shook her head as if trying to comprehend such a vicious thing. "How old were you?"

"Five." The admission usually brought a surge of bitterness, but there was just something about the way that she stared at him, into him, that made him feel more sad than anything else. And afraid. The way he'd felt as he'd stared at his mother's empty eyes and realized how cruel people could truly be.

"That's terrible."

" 'Tis nothing." He shrugged away from her and turned his attention to the framed drawing. "I see you have a new picture," he said, eager to move on to a different subject and shake the sudden surge of fear that filled him.

Pain.

Lust.

That's all he felt now. All he was capable of feeling. All he *wanted* to feel.

She stared at him a long moment, as if contemplating asking more questions. Finally, she seemed to think better of it. Her attention shifted back to the picture and she smiled. "This is my birthday present."

" 'Tis your birthday?"

"Actually, it was yesterday, but I forgot." Obviously she noticed his surprise. "I've been so busy lately, I haven't been able to think past this lab and Kara. But she remembered."

"A comely name."

"It was Gwen's second choice. She wanted Morgan, but her husband, Ed, went to grade school with a bully named Morgan. He said it brought back bad playground memories, so they went with Kara."

"Gwen?"

"She's my best friend." A cloud passed over her features. "*Was* my best friend. She was killed a few years back in a car accident. Ed was with her. The car was totaled."

She closed her eyes as if remembering. When she opened them, tears dotted her lashes. "Gwen was in and out of foster homes as a child—her single mother had given her up for adoption—and so she didn't have any real family to fall back on. Ed was an only child several years her senior. His mother had died when he was a teenager and his father had major heart problems and was living in a nursing home. There was no one for Kara, so Gwen named me her legal guardian."

"That's a hefty responsibility."

"It's a gift."

The warmth in her eyes as she glanced at the drawing touched something deep inside of him, beneath the stirring lust. A part of him he'd thought drained away along with his wife's life.

"I never really had anyone while I was growing up. My parents were always away working on some project or the other. They're both research scientists. My mother works for the Johnson Space Center and my father does work at MIT. She lives in Texas and he lives up north. They meet once a month to touch base. Sometimes in person. Other times they just use e-mail."

" 'Tis no way for a man and wife to live."

"Maybe so, but it's been their way for the past thirty-two years. Actually, they're closer now than they've ever been. When I was younger, my father spent six years in Iceland helping with a global-warming project. Then he was off to Russia for more global warming and a co-op project to help improve Russian agriculture. Then it was over to China to help engineer a chemically enhanced wheat product to feed the evergrowing population."

"When did you see him?"

"Holidays. Same time I saw my mother."

"Was she far away?"

"About five miles, but it might well have been five hundred. She was a workaholic. A woman who lived to work instead of worked to live." That familiar sadness touched her features. "She was always too busy for me, except when I was frustrating her. I was tarnishing the good Alexander image. She made time then."

"How did you frustrate her?"

"I would get in trouble at school, the principal would call, and she would come. Most of the time. Eventually, that stopped, as well, and she sent her secretary. And then she sent me to a special school so that no one would be calling her."

She shrugged. "That's when I met Gwen. I was fourteen. She was fifteen. I hated her on sight. She was nosey and a know-it-all. She kept after me so much that I finally buckled. We talked. We became friends. Best friends." She shook her head. "I can't let her down. I can't let Kara down. I have to make her better no matter what."

"Even if it costs you your soul?"

"Kara is my soul. If I lose her, I'll lose it anyway."

"That's ridiculous."

"I love her. There's nothing ridiculous about that."

"Trading your soul for a fool's notion *is* ridiculous."

"You've obviously never been in love."

"I'm not capable of it."

"What about the man you once were? Was he capable?"

"He was a fool. He didn't give a thought to the future. He lived for the moment and now I am paying the price."

"I can't lose Kara. I won't."

"There will be no turning back once the deal is complete. No changing your mind."

"Why are you trying to discourage me?"

Why was he trying?

Because his conscience was getting to him.

Because he always felt a moment's hesitation when dealing with his subjects.

Because he wanted her to be sure. She had to be sure for the deal to be complete.

Because he didn't want to hand her over to the Devil.

"It seems a terrible price to pay for a few drawings."

She glanced at the picture again and smiled. "Maybe for you, but I like flowers and pigs and smiley-face suns."

" 'Tis been a long time since I've seen the sun."

"How long?"

"Over one thousand years."

"That's terrible."

Hearing her say the words, seeing the incredulous look on her face, it actually felt terrible.

Images rushed at him and he thought of all the sunsets he'd watched on computer screens and television sets. How they'd filled him with such a tremendous sense of loss. Of longing. A feeling he'd quickly traded for the lust because it *was* terrible.

Remember who you are. What you are.

There was no longing. No more pain. No more loss. Only the furious drum of his heart, the quickening of his pulse, the throbbing of his groin.

"I like the darkness," he said, the words more for himself than her. "I've had some of my best times with nothing but a full moon overhead and a warm, willing woman beneath me." The words were true, but he said them more to shock her, to erase the look of compassion that burned so brightly in her eyes.

The only thing that burned as she stared back at him were her cheeks. They turned a bright pink, but her voice didn't so much as quiver when she replied, "I bet you have." She held her ground, as if she knew he meant to shock her and she didn't mean to let him.

"And how much would you bet?"

She shrugged. "I don't have anything left. My soul's already spoken for."

"But not your body." The words came out low and husky. Tempting.

"Tell me, sweet Sophie," he reached out and touched one strand of hair that framed her face, careful not to make contact with her skin. Not now. Not with his heart drumming so fast and his body burning so fiercely.

To touch her would be deadly to the plan, for Cain knew he wouldn't be able to stop with just a touch.

"Have you ever peeled off your clothes beneath a full moon and gone skinny-dipping on a hot summer's night? Then again, maybe you're more the indoor sort. With the full moon rushing through a window, your clothes in a puddle by the couch, your body naked and cool on the soft carpet? Or maybe you're on the couch, your skin against the bare leather while the darkness embraces you. Strokes you."

She stared up at him and a knowing light fired in her eyes. "You were there, weren't you?"

"And where is that?"

"My dreams. I saw you in my dreams. But it wasn't a dream, was it? It was real."

"I'm afraid," he rubbed her soft hair between his fingertips, "it was just a dream. For now."

"Forever." She shook her head and moved past him. "I don't have time for this." Laughter bubbled from her lips. "What am I thinking? I'm lusting after a spirit. A demon." She stared at him. "You're not real. You're not a man."

Join the Love Spell Romance Book Club
and **GET 2 FREE* BOOKS NOW–
An $11.98 value!**
Mail the Free* Book Certificate
Today!

Yes! I want to subscribe to the Love Spell Romance Book Club.

Please send me my **2 FREE* BOOKS**. I have enclosed $2.00 for shipping/handling. Every other month I'll receive the four newest Love Spell Romance selections to preview for 10 days. If I decide to keep them, I will pay the Special Members Only discounted price of just $4.49 each, a total of $17.96, plus $2.00 shipping/handling ($23.55 US in Canada). This is a **SAVINGS OF $6.00** off the bookstore price. There is no minimum number of books I must buy and I may cancel the program at any time. In any case, the **2 FREE* BOOKS** are mine to keep.

*In Canada, add $5.00 shipping and handling per order for the first shipment. For all future shipments to Canada, the cost of membership is $23.55 US, which includes shipping and handling.
(All payments must be made in US dollars.)

NAME: _____

ADDRESS: _____

CITY: _____ **STATE:** _____

COUNTRY: _____ **ZIP:** _____

TELEPHONE: _____

E-MAIL: _____

SIGNATURE: _____

If under 18, Parent or Guardian must sign. Terms, prices, and conditions subject to change. Subscription subject to acceptance. Dorchester Publishing reserves the right to reject any order or cancel any subscription.

The Best in Love Spell Romance!
Get Two Books Totally FREE*!

An $11.98 Value! FREE!

PLEASE RUSH
MY TWO FREE
BOOKS TO ME
RIGHT AWAY!

Enclose this card with $2.00
in an envelope and send to:

Love Spell Romance Book Club
20 Academy Street
Norwalk, CT 06850-4032

He wasn't, yet there was just something about hearing her say the words out loud that both angered and saddened him at the same time.

And made him all the more determined to prove her wrong.

"I must be crazy. Imagine thinking of you *that* way. It's absurd. It's insane. It's—"

Her words stalled when Cain reached out and pulled her into his arms. And then he did what he'd been wanting to do since the first moment he'd looked upon her.

He kissed her.

Chapter Nine

She was dreaming again.

He was too potent, too intoxicating to be real.

His mouth ate at hers. The hot tip of his tongue stroked her bottom lip and coaxed her mouth open. With a soft cry, she gave in. He plunged deep, feeding from her, drawing the air from her lungs only to give it back, sustaining her as he ravaged with the potency of his kiss.

A kiss as life-affirming as Heaven.

As sinful as Hell.

Strong arms gathered her close, pulling her flush against him. Hard muscle met soft flesh. He burned her with his heat, melting the stiffness in her body. She leaned into him, molding to each hard contour, relishing the heat that sank into her and warmed her from the inside out.

She grew hotter, more desperate, her nerves buzzing from the feel of his body, the plunder of his mouth. Need flowered inside her, spreading through her body, gripping every inch until her thought processes short-circuited and she ached and burned. She couldn't think much less resist.

Resist.

The word whispered through her mind, but it wasn't loud enough to drown out the frantic beat of his heart pounding against her breasts, the raw moan that vibrated from his lips, into her mouth, a sound that was both passion and possession.

His hands swept down her shoulder blades. His fingertips trailed down her spine, gliding purposefully over her buttocks. He cupped her bottom, kneading and lifting until she felt the full weight of his arousal pressing into her.

The sensation sent a wash of heat through her, burning her up from the inside out. Her skin prickled and screamed from the heat. Her body ached.

She wanted him.

The truth bubbled up inside her.

Higher, higher . . .

Hotter, hotter . . .

Her arms wound around his neck and she

pressed herself against him, desperate to feel more, to meld with him until he pushed everything else aside and filled her up. Until she felt nothing but him. No desperation or longing or fear.

Crazy!

She'd known a man's touch.

A man's kiss.

A man's possession.

But nothing and no one had ever affected her like this.

Because he was *more than a man.*

She knew the truth, yet her feelings ruled at the moment and he really and truly *felt* like a man.

Hard. Muscular. Aroused.

For a few breathless, heartpounding moments, the world fell away as Cain filled her every sense.

She forgot all about her formula. About the desperation that lived and breathed inside her. About her job and her responsibilties. She was no longer a godmother or a scientist.

She was a woman in need of a man.

This man.

"You feel so warm," he murmured against her lips. "So very warm and I have been cold for much too long."

She knew the feeling. She'd felt the coldness, the emptiness, the sheer loneliness.

"So have I," she breathed.

He pulled away and stared deep into her eyes.

Flames lept in the dark, vibrant depths of his gaze as looked at her, into her. She knew in an instant that he saw every emotion whirling inside her. That he felt them as potently as she did.

"I want you, Sophie." Sincerity rang in his voice and touched something deep inside her.

The inkling of worry and doubt that lingered in her mind quickly fled, swamped by the desire that rushed through her. She found herself nodding.

"I—" she started to repeat his words back to him, but his mouth claimed hers again in a quick, almost violent kiss. Their tongues tangled, their breaths stalled, their hearts pounded . . .

"No!"

The fierce denial echoed in her ears a heartbeat before Cain thrust her away from him.

She stumbled back against the edge of the counter. Her fingers grasped at the smooth formica, searching for a stronghold. Her legs trembled and her insides quivered and balance was a faraway notion.

"What's wrong?"

"I . . ." He swallowed, his body trembling with the small effort. "I . . ." The words wouldn't come.

"Cain? What is it?"

His mouth opened, but he didn't say anything. He simply shook his head. "We should get to work," he finally barked, his chest heaving, his nostrils flaring.

Even as he said the words, he didn't turn toward the lab station, he simply stared at her.

Emotion warred in his gaze and she knew that he fought some internal battle.

"I shouldn't have done that," he told her.

"I wanted you to. I wouldn't have let you if I didn't want it."

"Let me?" A bitter smile touched his lips. "You had no choice."

"I always have a choice. I wanted what happened. I just didn't realize how much until it did happen."

"You and every other woman," he said. He shook his head. "Do not fool yourself. You wanted me because all women want me."

"O-kay." She licked her lips and eyed him. "So all women want a demon? Funny, but the last time I looked, I didn't think 'demon' was listed as one the top ten female fantasies."

"I am not an ordinary demon, Sophie. I am . . ." The words failed him as pain contorted his features. He arched his back and his legs seemed to buckle and he fell to his knees as if stricken by some invisible hand.

Sophie was next to him in the next instant, reaching for him. "What's wrong?"

"Nothing," he ground out.

"You're sick."

He shook his head. "No. It's . . ." He ground

his teeth and let out a pain-filled hiss.

"You are. You're sick. Here," she reached for his hand, her fingers closing around his. Her palm came into contact with his and it was as if he'd been hit by a bolt of electricity.

He went rigid. His gaze snapped to hers and horror filled his eyes.

"Cain? What is it? What's wrong . . ." The question faded in a rush of pain as his grip on her hand tightened.

He looked at her, but he didn't see her. He saw something else entirely as his eyes grew a vibrant, pulsing green. They mesmerized like an up close view of a tornado, picking her up and whirling her. Her heart pounded, her blood rushed and fear filled her.

"Please," she finally managed.

The one word seemed to pierce whatever barrier surrounded him. Recognition filled his eyes and his grip eased. He blinked and let go of her hand. His body shook as he leaned over and gasped for air.

"Are you all right?"

He didn't respond for a long moment. He drank in air, his chest heaving, his body shaking.

She couldn't help herself. She reached out, her hand settling on his shoulder.

He stiffened and pushed her away. "We're wasting time," he said, his words raw and deep. He climbed to his feet and Sophie followed.

"You should sit down."

"I'm fine."

"You don't look fine."

"I'm fine."

"I don't believe that. I saw you just now—" Her words stalled as he turned and she ran into his chest.

He set her away from him immediately and stepped back, but it was too late. Her heart started to pound and desire rushed through her and all from just a few seconds of contact.

Her gaze riveted on his lips and she couldn't help it. She licked her own, suddenly desperate for another kiss, another chance to forget her life and her sanity for a few precious moments.

Moments?

She wanted to forget for even longer, because she didn't want just one kiss. She wanted him and everything he'd offered such a short time ago.

The past rushed at her and she could still feel his hardness pressed against the cradle of her thighs, his hands on her buttocks, her fingertips trailing the hard, delicious length of him . . .

Geez, had she lost her mind? She'd actually touched him. Hell, she'd been close to doing not only that, but much more. Just one button and the swift slide of a zipper away from losing her focus over a man.

More than a man.

Sophie had always had a weakness for dark

and dangerous. Mr. Right Now, rather than Mr. Right. She certainly couldn't get more *right now* than Cain, or more dark and dangerous as far as bad boys went. He was a spirit, for Pete's sake.

A demon.

Bad with a capital B.

With him there was no possibility of a long-term relationship. No marriage or kids or the proverbial two-story house with the white picket fence.

No future.

Temporary.

Not to mention he was handsome. Mesmerizing. And boy, could he kiss.

No, he wasn't an ordinary man by any means, and so she'd been overwhelmed.

Understanding the situation, however, in no way eased the guilt that rushed through her. She became instantly aware of her open shirt. Clutching the edges together, she started to work at the buttons.

He was temporary and her insanity was temporary, and it was over. She had responsibilities. She had Kara. She didn't have time for this.

"This isn't a good idea," she said, turning away from him."

" 'Tis a terrible idea," he agreed.

"It's not you," she rushed on, eager for a distraction from the frantic pounding of her own heart. "I mean, it is you. Partly. You're the exact sort of guy that I go for. *If* you were a guy," she rushed on, realizing her mistake. "you'd be the exact sort I would fall for, but you're not. Which is all the more reason that I'm attracted to you."

Silence settled between them as she slid the last button into place. She turned to face him and found him staring at her, a look that was a cross between pleasure and pain on his face.

"You're attracted to me," he stated. "But of course you're attracted to me."

"This can't happen," she went on. "I mean, it's the principle of the thing. Women simply don't fall for a demon. Not to mention, there are the physical drawbacks. Why, it might not even be possible for you to . . . I mean, I know you have all the equipment. I felt it. But maybe you can't really use it."

"I can use it," he assured her, looking suddenly amused that she would even consider the possibility that he couldn't. "I am fully capable. Make no mistake about that."

"I just thought . . . I mean, you're not a man, but at the same time, you're every man I've ever gone after. The quintessential rebel. That's why I'm attracted. It's not really you, it's everything you represent. You see, I've got this weakness for—" The words stalled in her throat as her gaze fixed on a nearby file cabinet where she stored her diskettes.

An unlocked file cabinet.

The top drawer stood slightly open, an inch of darkness creeping from inside.

"You are far from weak, Sophie Alexander. You are a strong woman. Your attraction isn't from weakness. Perhaps, it is me and not this type you speak of that you are attracted to . . . What is wrong?"

His question barely penetrated the fear that drummed at her temples as her gaze lingered on the open drawer before shifting to his. Her stomach knotted and her chest tightened and she knew.

"Someone broke into my lab."

"Tell me once more. What time did you leave last night?"

"I didn't leave last night. It was early this morning. I worked late and then fell asleep on the couch. The place was already buzzing by the time I left. There were people everywhere."

"Could it have happened while you were asleep? Maybe before you left? Maybe you just now noticed it."

She shook her head. "No. It happened after I left. I'm sure of it. I never leave the drawer unlocked unless I'm retrieving a diskette or some old notes. I unlock it, get what I need out and lock it back."

"So you're saying you never leave it unlocked? Even when you're here?"

"That's right. I'm careful. I've always been

careful when it comes to my work. I lost the background notes for an entire formula back when I first started in Research and Development. Since then, I've been paranoid. I back everything up, put everything in its place. That way there are no mistakes."

"Everybody makes mistakes."

"Not me. Not this time—"

"Ohmygod!" Carol's excited voice carried from the doorway and Sophie turned to see her boss rush toward her. "I knew it. I just knew it! I want him arrested right now."

"Calm down, ma'am. Do you know the perpetrator?"

"Jeffrey Taylor. His address is—"

"How do you know he's the person responsible for this?"

"Trust me. I just know."

"Do you have evidence?"

"He's a suspicious character."

"Says who? Has he done or said anything?"

"He lives and breathes. Look, Officer, Jeff is a sorry sonofabitch and this is exactly something he would do."

"I'm afraid being an SOB doesn't make him guilty of this crime. If there was a crime. We still haven't established an actual break-in. There's no signs of a forced entry. Nothing missing."

"That's because I didn't leave my diskettes in

here like I usually do. I took them home with me. And my laptop."

"You work an awful lot, Miss Alexander."

"This is an important project," Carol chimed in. "This is going to make or break us this year."

"When I'm near a deadline, I do work a lot after hours."

"That probably doesn't leave too much time for sleeping."

"What are you getting at?" Carol asked.

"Just that Miss Alexander here might have inadvertently left the cabinet open. She's tired. Overworked. She probably forgot—"

"I didn't forget. I never forget." Even with an emergency page, she'd taken the time to slam the drawer shut, and push the lock into place this morning when she'd rushed home to Kara.

"There's always a first time. How are you doing over there, Wesley?"

"Only one set of prints so far."

"He's got prints?" Carol's eyes lit with excitement.

"One set. Probably Miss Alexander's." The detective eyed Sophie. "We'll need your prints to match with what we've found. If we find any that are unidentifiable, then we'll move to the next step."

"Listen, Officer, I wouldn't have stepped up security if I wasn't one hundred percent positive that something funny was going on."

"I'm afraid your instincts don't count as evidence. Look, I'll file a report, but if we don't find any proof of anything out of the ordinary, we can't do anything more."

"I understand."

"Well, I don't," Carol said, following the officer to the door. "You're the police. You're supposed to protect innocent people and I'm an innocent person. My business was burglarized and you tell me you can't do anything? Does this sound right to you? I'm calling my congressman. Better yet, I'm calling your boss."

"I'll get him on the phone for you."

The door shut behind Carol and the investigating officer. Footsteps and muffled voices sounded on the other side of the door before fading.

"Only one set of prints," Officer Wesley announced as he dusted the last few inches of the cabinet. "We're going to dust the keypad out in the hall to be sure, but so far nothing really looks suspicious."

Maybe she *had* left it unlocked. She'd been in a hurry this morning. Panicked. She could have overlooked it and simply assumed that she'd locked it because she always did.

That's what reason told her, but the hair standing on end on the back of her neck said something altogether. She just had this feeling that someone had invaded her personal space. That she'd been violated.

Yes, someone had definitely been in her lab.
But who?
And more importantly, why?

"What do you think you're doing?" the Evil One demanded as Cain found himself jerked from the darkness and suspended within the center of a circle of fire. The flames licked and crackled, pushing back the darkness just enough and casting an eerie glow on the Evil One's perfect features.

He looked a true prince of darkness tonight, with his long, flowing black robe. His hair was also long and black and he sported a matching goatee that made him look all the more sinister.

Yet it wasn't the devil himself that frightened Cain. It was the darkness. The nothingness. The void just beyond the flames that awaited him.

"Foreplay," Cain replied, desperate to ignore the truth vibrating through him. He still burned for Sophie, and all because of a kiss.

That's all he'd meant to give her. One swift kiss to prove to her that he was every bit as real as any man.

He wasn't. A fact that had never bothered him until she'd said the words that had driven him to prove her wrong and kiss her until she responded to him the way a woman responds to a man.

"You disobeyed my orders."

"How so? Foreplay precedes sex. I'm merely

laying the groundwork for a full-blown seduction later on. She'll be so needy by the time the formula is finished, she will hand over anything I ask of her."

The Evil One stared at him, his eyes like twin mirrors that reflected the bright orange flames.

And in the center of the fire, Cain saw his own reflection. There was no mistaking the fierce set of jaw, the taut lines of his neck, the brightness in his eyes.

He was the one primed and ready. The one so needy that he would hand over anything for one more kiss, one more touch.

"Do not disobey me, Cain."

"Have I ever?"

"You've never been on an assignment like this, and how does the saying go? There's a first time for everything."

"Not for me, and this is no different from any other assignment. It's just taking a little longer and patience isn't my strong suit. I should think you would understand that."

He smiled, a cold tilt to his lips that might have sent a chill through Cain if he hadn't been so worked up. "Speaking of patience, how much longer?"

"We're close."

"Get closer."

"That's what I was doing."

"You know what I mean." A benevolent smile came over his face and if Cain hadn't known better, he would have sworn that the Evil One felt compassion. "I know how hard women can be to resist sometimes. I, too, have been at a woman's mercy. It wasn't pretty. But, ah, she was." He closed his eyes as if seeing something in his mind's eye. "A shame she had to stand against me." His eyes opened and drilled into Cain. "I don't like to be challenged or bested. I can't be." He lifted his hand.

Cain felt a pressure against his chest, then a piercing cold like the tip of a knife. It sliced into him and a cold draft of air snaked around his heart.

"You don't have a heart, dear boy. Remember that. *Remember*."

The sensation blinded him and then it was gone. Cain opened his eyes to find himself back in Sophie's lab. The room was now empty, the police having already left. They'd escorted Sophie out and Cain hadn't had a chance to say goodbye.

Or to kiss her again.

He shook away the parting thought and turned his attention to the computer screen.

The monitor flickered and the Riveria appeared, the water a deep, inviting blue. The sun sparkled off the surface, promising a warmth he hadn't felt in a long, long time.

If ever.

The thought whispered through his mind and images tried to push their way through. Mem-

169

ories. Of death. Destruction. Darkness.

He punched a button on the screen, determined to draw the scene in closer, to focus on the half-naked women strutting across the white sand. The screen flickered and the screen saver appeared.

He went to punch the button again, but the picture stopped him. It was a photograph of a petite blonde wearing a pink princess Halloween costume. She held a plastic pumpkin overflowing with candy. But she wasn't standing outside a house, ready to head up the walk to Trick or Treat.

Instead, she sat upright in a hospital bed, an IV tube hooked to her arm. Paper pumpkins decorated the wall behind her and a black rubber spider dangled from a nearby heart monitor.

He looked closer and noted the dark circles under her eyes, her hair thin beneath the princess hat. She was ill, yet she still smiled for the camera. For the person behind the camera.

Sophie.

This was Kara. The sick child. Sophie's goddaughter. The reason she'd sold her soul to the devil.

"Crazy," he muttered, but it wasn't so crazy. Cain himself had sacrificed his soul for someone else. He knew what motivated a person to forget everything save one driving force—be it life or death.

Yes, he knew, all too well and it was a mistake he didn't intend to repeat.

Never, *ever* again.

He was here to do a job, despite what the future held.

He closed his eyes against the memory of the vision. He'd seen Sophie's future. For that split-second, when he'd been fighting his lust and she'd been trying to help him, she'd touched his hand with hers and he'd seen.

She'd been crying and begging for her life.

For her soul.

But the Evil One had already taken it from her.

Shaking his head, he forced the image aside. He was merely here to do a job and he intended to do it, despite the doubts lingering in his mind.

It wasn't his choice. It was hers.

One she'd already made.

Chapter Ten

Someone was following her.

Sophie tried to slow her pounding heart as she stopped at the crosswalk and waited for the light to change. She was nervous and jittery from the burglary at the lab.

The *supposed* burglary. The police didn't seem to suspect anything. They thought she'd left the drawer unlocked and her own notes in disarray.

Maybe. While she had always been methodical and thorough—traits she'd inherited from her parents despite her best efforts to the contrary—she certainly wasn't incapable of breaching routine and making a mistake. With the enormous amount of stress she'd been under

172

lately, it would stand to reason that she might behave out of character.

That's what reason told her. But the strange fluttering in her stomach and the goosebumps chasing up and down her arms said something altogether different.

The light changed and she started across the street. She kept her gaze focused in front of her, her ears tuned to the surrounding sounds; the buzz of traffic, the murmur of passing voices, the bluesy wail of a saxophone from a nearby jazz bar, the steady thump of footsteps . . .

Her head snapped around, her gaze searching the faces that surrounded her. There was a couple who held hands walking a few feet back, their attention fixed on one another. A harried looking woman carrying two sacks of groceries. A biker wearing spandex shorts and a biking helmet rolled his bike behind her. A man wearing a three-piece suit, talking on a cell phone rushed past her, his shoulder bumping up against hers and pushing her slightly to the side.

Of course she heard footsteps. She was surrounded by people, at least for the next few blocks as she made her way down Michigan Avenue.

Sophie held on to that knowledge and forced herself to calm down. *Just walk.*

She drew in a deep breath and took step by

173

step, her attention fixed on the man who rolled the bicycle just up ahead. She'd always wanted time to take up bicycling. Maybe when she and Kara moved to the country, she would do just that. They could both get bikes and ride all over Gruene. Through the main part of town. Down every dirt road. Across the open pastures.

The thought made her smile and she managed to relax for the next few blocks, until the crowd surrounding her started to dwindle. The couple turned at the next corner. The businessman stopped off at a local deli. The woman with groceries fumbled for her key before mounting the steps of a small brownstone on the right-hand side. The biker eventually climbed onto his cycle and started to peddle, taking the corner just up ahead at a frightening speed.

Sophie found herself alone, her own footsteps echoing in her head.

Clop, clop. Clop, clop. Clop, clop, clop—

The extra beat sent a burst of fear through her and she whirled, her gaze darting at the empty street behind her. The streetlights glowed overhead and noise echoed in the distance, but there was nothing nearby. Only the buzz of the lights overhead and the faint noises coming from inside the surrounding apartments.

Sophie focused on her building just up ahead and the doorway. She picked up her steps and walked faster.

Clop, clop. Clop, clop. Clop, clop, clop . . .

She started to run, her briefcase slapping against her hip as she raced up the street and mounted the steps to her building.

"Miss Alexander?" Sam, the night doorman got to his feet the minute she burst into the door. "What's wrong."

"Nothing." Sophie gasped for air. "I just got a little spooked, I think."

He passed her, a frown on his face, as he made his way to the door. He peered out. "I don't see anything."

"I'm sure it was just my imagination." She walked into the elevator and punched the button for her floor, and left Sam staring after her with a concerned look on his face.

Imagination.

That's what she wanted to believe. What she did her damndest to convince herself of as she rode the elevator up to her floor. Unfortunately, her heart pounded just a little too fast and her skin crawled with uneasiness and the hair on her arms stood on end.

Because someone *had* been following her.

Again, she couldn't help but wonder who and why?

"Come on, Luke. Go easy on the poor girl."

The Evil One turned to see the tall, slender woman who stood nearby. The street light beamed overhead. A circle of light spilled down around her, surrounding her. She had hair so blond it was almost silver, her eyes as warm and as comforting as hot cocoa on a cold, blistery winter day.

Not that the Evil One had experienced anything cold or comforting in a very, *very* long time. But in the far, most distant recess of his jaded soul, the memory lingered.

Like the bad taste after biting into a spoiled apple.

At least, that's what he told himself whenever he crossed paths with Celeste.

He shrugged and forced his gaze away from the woman to the apartment building across the street. His attention shifted to the tenth floor in time to see the drapes swish shut as Sophie Alexander blocked out any prying eyes.

Or so she thought, but the Evil One knew better. Sophie couldn't so easily shut out what hunted her.

He caught a fleeting glimpse of her tear-streaked face, her fear-filled eyes as she peeked past the edge of the window covering and scoured the street below.

Her gaze lingered on him a split-second, but he knew she didn't see him. He didn't want her to and thy will be done, or so the saying went.

"That refers to someone a little higher up." Celeste's voice penetrated his thoughts and he frowned. "Yes, I can read your thoughts, Luke. You aren't so special, though you think you are."

He forced his best smile and resisted the urge to step forward and slide his hands around the slim column of her throat. That, or kiss her.

"Ah, but I wouldn't let you kiss me."

"Not now, but there was a time."

"Temporary insanity," she said. Her gaze shifted from his, despite his best efforts to keep her focused.

He couldn't, for Celeste wasn't mortal, and she wasn't susceptible to his charm.

But there was a time . . .

"Stop reminiscing and fess up. You're tormenting that poor girl."

"Don't remind me."

"It wasn't me."

"Tell that to someone who doesn't know you as well as I do."

"*Did* know me. It's been a long time."

He arched an eyebrow at her and let his gaze rove her from head to toe, drinking in every luscious curve. His gaze lingered on her face and the small groove where her face dimpled when she smiled. "Perhaps I've changed."

"Perhaps you've given up your fear tactics in favor of playing fair?" She shook her head. "Next thing you'll tell me, you've opened up a ski resort right in the middle of Hades."

"Now there's an idea."

She smiled, her lips parting in a brilliant show of straight, white teeth. But it was more than just the expression that sent a burst of longing through him. It was the softening of her eyes and the way her dimple creased her smooth skin.

"You can't fool me. You never could. You just refuse to admit it. I know you. Your every step. What makes you tick. Greed."

"Such was once the same for you."

She shook her head. "You assumed I wanted the same things because I listened to your dreams. I never shared them."

"Really?" He circled her, his gaze traveling the length of her, from her flaxen hair to her bare feet peeking from chic sandals. She looked like any other woman walking the streets of Chicago.

Far from a divine being.

"I seem to recall a time when you enjoyed the darkness as much as me. When you liked peeling off your robes and dancing beneath a full moon." He wanted so much to touch her, to see if she felt as soft as she once did. To see if her hair slipped through his fingers like fine strands of silken thread.

Never again.

"I was young and foolish. We all were. Once. You still are."

"You truly think the worst of me, don't you?"

"I have every reason to." She eyed him. "Leave her alone. She's facing enough without you making the situation all the more difficult."

"She came to me. Which makes me wonder

why you're here. Don't tell me, she's two-timing the both of us."

"An interested third party, and do me a favor, back off."

"We're talking favors now, are we? And what favor will you give me in return?"

"Can't a clear conscience be enough?" Even as she asked the question, she seemed to realize its absurdity. "What am I saying?" She shook her head, disgust and disappointment evident in her expression.

In another lifetime, in his lifetime, he might have been offended by her look.

In another lifetime.

"Leave her be," she said again. The light brightened, forcing him back a few steps and blinding him.

When his eyes opened, she was gone, the street lamp was dark and the shadows closed around him once more.

Back off . . . As if he would heed her ridiculous request. As if he could.

Oddly enough, even he had told the truth. He wasn't the one stalking Sophie Alexander.

But he knew who was, and it was going to take a lot more than a warning to stop the soul responsible.

He'd made her nervous tonight.

He hadn't meant to. He'd meant to get close enough to have a look at her progress. To learn

179

the layout of her laboratory, the whereabouts of her notes, her recordkeeping system for tracking experiments and results.

He'd meant to shut the drawer and leave things exactly as found, but he'd been too excited by his discovery.

By God, she was close. So damned close.

Which meant he had to stay close.

She knew he was there. She didn't know who, of course. She would never know who, not until it was too late.

She would regret shutting him out and turning her back. He would make sure of that.

In the meantime . . .

Close.

Very close.

"She's doing good," Sophie told Dr. Stevens later that evening during his nightly phone call. "Holding steady."

"That's good, but I still want to see her in here on Friday morning for her weekly blood workup. I've also been wanting to talk to you about a new preventative therapy program."

"A new drug?"

"And a mild form of radiation. We're taking a pro-active approach with laser treatments now using a seek and destroy method."

"No more radiation." Images of Kara sick and weak pushed into her head. Tears burned her eyes and she shook her head. "She barely made it through the chemo the last time. I don't want to do that to her again."

"You won't have a choice. As I've said time and time again, remission is only temporary."

"Not this time."

"What's that supposed to mean? Have you made some headway with your research?"

"A little." She wanted to tell him everything, but something held her back. A superstition that if she blurted out everything she might jinx herself. It was all so unbelievable and to say it out loud would make it even more so.

"I know it's temporary," she went on, "but it could be temporary as in several years. People do stay in remission that long."

"Yes, there are the exceptions. Kara could be one, as well, which is why you can't let this opportunity slip by. She's feeling better. She's stronger. She's a perfect candidate for preventative treatment. It's been very successful with the test group so far."

Desperation pushed her to ask, "How successful?"

"A twenty percent drop in abnormal cell count."

"Twenty percent?"

"That's a substantial decrease. Enough to prolong remission and put off the inevitable for over half the group. Most were facing death not six months ago and now they have a substantial increase in time."

"But no cure."

"There isn't now and will never be a cure, Sophie. Not in our lifetime. Not in Kara's. You have to be a realist and take what you can get."

"Not at Kara's expense."

"At least think about it. You need to do something before the remission ends and it's too late."

"That's exactly what I'm trying to do," she murmured to herself as she hung up the phone and went to check on Kara.

She was standing in the doorway to the child's room, staring at the girl's sleeping form when she felt the presence behind her.

Her heart raced forward and her stomach tightened and she jerked around.

"Umph . . ." Cain's groan echoed through the room as Sophie landed a punch to his rock-hard abdomen.

"Geez, you scared the daylights out of me."

"I didn't mean to." He massaged his abdomen and she remembered what he'd said about feeling things more intensely than a real man.

"I didn't mean to hit you. I'm sorry."

"You were defending yourself. 'Tis normal. You did not know it was me."

"I did. I mean, I almost did, but I've been a ball of nerves since the lab. And then the walk from the parking garage."

"What happened?"

"Nothing, yet . . . I don't know. I just feel like

182

somebody's watching me." She frowned. "It doesn't help to have you sneaking up on me."

"I never sneak." His gaze went past her. "She looks much better, does she not?"

"Yes." She shifted her gaze and eyed him. "But how do you know she looks better . . ." She let her question fade as she shook her head. "One of the satanic Six Pack, I'm sure."

"I saw her picture at your office on your computer. The screen saver."

She smiled, seeing the image in her mind. "Anything would be better than that. She was right in the middle of her chemotherapy last year when that was taken. She was feeling very sick and weak, but not too sick to get dressed up. She couldn't eat any candy, but I quickly learned that it doesn't matter if you can eat candy or not, you need it for Halloween. I wheeled her from nurses' station to nurses' station until her pumkin was full and she was too tired to keep her eyes open. It wasn't a traditional Halloween, but we made the best of it." She eyed Kara. "That's the story of her life. Always making the best of whatever comes her way. She deserves a few good things, don't you think?" She didn't wait for his answer. She walked into the room, pulled the cover up over Kara's shoulder and kissed her cheek. Soft skin met her lips and the scent of strawberry shampoo and bubble-gum lip gloss filled her nostrils and made her smile.

A few seconds later, she pulled the door almost closed and walked past Cain toward the living room.

"Your birthday party?" he asked when he saw the party hat sitting on the coffee table.

Sophie dropped down to the couch and picked up the hat. Leaning back into the cushions, she stared at the paper contraption. "It was a surprise party. Kara loves parties as much as she loves holidays. Any excuse to eat cake and have goodies and get dressed up, be it a costume or a fancy dress. For St. Patrick's Day last year, we actually painted our faces green to go with the green T-shirts that she insisted we wear. It was just around the house, but it was fun." The past rushed at her and she smiled. "Gwen was the same way. I remember that she actually spray-painted her hair silver for President's Day back in college. She even went to class that way."

"What about you?"

"I was right there with her, always ready to do any and everything. That's one thing we had in common. We were never afraid to defy the norm. Of course, we did it for different reasons back then. Gwen was just out to have fun."

"And you?"

"Anything to go against the grain. The more outlandish things I did, the more my parents shook their head and rolled their eyes."

"You wanted to displease them."

"Better a head shake and an eye roll than

184

nothing." Her gaze met his. "At least I knew they were noticing me." She fingered the party hat. "Otherwise I was non-existent." She traced the bright pink Barbie insignia. "This was my second surprise party. My first was the first year that I met Gwen. She made a cake and invited the other girls on our dorm floor. They all jumped out and yelled surprise and nearly scared me half to death. That was my first birthday party."

"Your first surprise party," he corrected.

"No, that was my first birthday party. My parents weren't much for celebrating. When they remembered, they didn't have time for such nonsense. After all, what is one cake in the big thick of things? I understand where they were coming from now, but I didn't then. I was just a kid."

"Who wanted a birthday cake."

She nodded. "And a present. And one of these silly party hats."

"Well, now you have it."

"Now I do." And she intended to keep it all. To keep Kara. "So what about the mighty Vikings? Do they throw pretty cool birthday parties?"

"I'm no longer a Viking."

"So who are you now?"

"Satan's spawn."

"Tell that to someone who hasn't seen you wearing a pink Barbie birthday hat."

At her words, he reached up and pulled the hat from his head. A grin curved his lips and she couldn't help herself, she smiled back at him.

"Feasts," he finally said. "We used to celebrate with food. Lots of food." She arched an eyebrow at him and he went on, "To a Viking, every new year is cause for celebration. Every day where one continues to walk and talk and live is a joyous event."

"So the Vikings revered life."

"Some did, some didn't."

"What about you?"

He shrugged. "I did and I didn't."

"What does that mean?"

"There were times that I revered life, and other times where I merely wanted it to end. And still other times where it had to continue so that I could continue. So that I could finish what I'd set out to do."

"Which was?"

"Kill a man," he replied. "My one mission in life before I lost my life."

"Why?"

He simply stared at her then. "No one's ever asked me why."

"I'm asking."

"I had to kill him."

"Why?"

Silence settled around them and she didn't think he was going to answer. Instead, he stared at the hat sitting in his lap. "Because he killed my wife."

"You were married?"

He nodded. "Once. A long, long time ago. For a short time. A peaceful time."

"I'm sorry."

"Don't be. It's over and done with."

"So you avenged her death. That's what brought you here."

"Not revenge. It wasn't my motive that landed me in service to the Evil One. It was my lack of remorse. It wasn't just my duty. I enjoyed what I did."

"I would have too if it had been my wife. You must have loved her very much."

"It wasn't about love. I took a vow to protect her and I failed. I failed her, but she never failed me. She saved my life once and I owed her. She was unjustly killed, so I killed on her behalf. I set things right and I enjoyed doing so."

"Sounds like love to me."

"Love is a useless emotion. Lust is much better.

"Lust doesn't nurse you when you're sick, or remember your birthday or rub your feet after a long day's work, or listen when you need to talk. Love does that. Someone *in* love."

"And what about the nights when you want more? When your body aches and burns and you need a man so badly you can't stand it?"

"The person I love will be there."

"Not always. The world has a way of twisting things around and taking them away when you least expect it."

"I don't agree with that. I think we all make our own choices, our own destiny, so to speak. There's always *something* you can do."

"Not always. Sometimes it's out of your control and there's nothing you can do. No way to turn back. To undo a wrong or finish a right." The shadow that crossed his face had her reaching out before she could stop herself.

As if he needed her comfort.

He's not a man. He doesn't need a man's comfort.

But she touched him anyway because, at that moment, he looked like a man, and when she touched his skin and felt the hair-roughened warmth beneath her palm, he felt like a man. And when his gaze locked with hers, she knew he *felt* like a man, his gaze bright with anger and a loneliness she knew all too well.

"You must have endured a lot to be so bitter."

"I endured hatred. Fear. Repulsion. From the moment I was born."

"I'm sorry."

"Don't be. It was a long, *long* time ago."

"Obviously not because you still feel the fallout from it."

"I don't feel anything." He stared at her and fixed his gaze on her lips. The familiar beast roared to life inside him and he smiled his most seductive smile. "I take that back. I feel one thing."

She let her hand fall away, as if disappointed at the sudden transformation. "I guess we really should get to work."

He resisted the urge to kiss her and prove just what he felt, for greater than his desire was the need to erase the sudden disappointment from her gaze.

"My thoughts exactly."

Chapter Eleven

She was dreaming again.

She told herself that as she raced through the darkness, her heart pounding a furious rythmn. The footsteps echoed around her. They were behind her, in front of her, beside her . . . She whipped around, searching the darkness, but she couldn't find the source.

Still, she knew someone was there, following her, watching her.

Tears streamed down her face as she kept running, desperate to get away, to find safety, to stop the thundering footsteps that echoed in her ear.

A dream, she told herself over and over again. Just a dream.

No matter how the wind whipped at her—

nipping and biting at her flesh, drawing goosebumps that chased up and down her arms—the hard, cold concrete scraped at the soles of her bare feet. She breathed, drawing in oxygen, desperate for a deep, calming breath that wouldn't come.

She was running too fast, her heart racing, her blood pumping.

Faster. Faster.

I'm coming for you, Sophie. I'm coming . . .

She didn't need to hear the deep, throbbing voice to know he was close. She could hear the presence behind her, smell the danger in the air, feel the threat. She moved quickly, but her pursuer didn't slow his pace. He kept coming, dogging her, wearing her down until she stumbled, unable to go on.

"Please," she whispered as the footsteps closed in.

The smell grew stronger, burning her nostrils as she closed her eyes and waited for the inevitable.

Fear. Pain. *Death*.

She wasn't sure how she knew what he meant to do to her, but she did. What she didn't know was why.

"Why are you doing this?" she cried, needing to understand. "What do you want from me?"

"Everything . . ."

Dread gripped her nerve endings and sheer terror paralyzed her bones. She tried to move, to fight back, but he was too strong.

Out of the pitch black came a pair of dark, gloved hands. They grasped at her, one snaking around her neck, the other covering her mouth. They squeezed, cutting off her air supply, making her squirm as her unseen attacker's hold grew tighter and death loomed closer.

"Sophie."

She heard Cain's deep, rich voice and it soothed the fear beating in her chest. She forced her eyes open to the impenetrable blackness and found a small pinpoint of light just up ahead. Blinking, her gaze focused and the pinpoint became a face.

Cain stared back at her, his eyes a bright, gleaming green, his hair a direct contrast to the darkness around them. He stood like a beacon in the night, ready to guide her to safety if she could just break free of the gloved hands.

Her gaze locked with his and she felt his warmth even from such a fierce distance. She drew it in, closing her eyes as the feeling rushed through her body from her head to her toes.

"We are one now," his voice whispered. Her hands lifted, but they weren't her hands. They looked and felt the same, but they were strong, fused by the power vibrating inside her.

Cain.

Her attacker's grip loosened and fell away, and Sophie found her legs lifting, racing forward with a renewed vigor. She felt her own heart pumping, the sound echoed by another thump.

Cain.

They moved forward, until the darkness softened and Sophie found herself back in her living room. The moon lit up the sky just outside the large bay window overlooking the river. The light pushed its way into the room, shoving back the shadows to the far corners.

Her hands trembled with a power all their own and her body quivered and she closed her eyes, trying to understand what was happening.

We are one.

His deep voice echoed in her head a heartbeat before the warmth seeped away and she was cold again.

Alone.

She opened her eyes to find Cain standing in front of her now. So close, yet not nearly as close as he had been a few moments before.

One.

"I shouldn't have done that." The words came out as little more than a raw, husky whisper laced with regret.

His shoulders shook, the muscles in his arms bulging, as if it was all he could do to stand before her and hold himself in check.

As if he held back on purpose, not wanting to touch her, hold her, comfort her.

Crazy.

Cain didn't hold back. He'd been the first one

to tantalize and tease and overwhelm her senses when all she'd wanted was to concentrate on her experiments.

At least in real life.

In her fantasies, however, she'd had less misgivings about indulging in a little sensual pleasure. The fantasies were preferable to the dreams of death and destruction she'd had for so long should she fail with her formula.

Now she had nightmares of what would come should she succeed, of what fate would befall her courtesy of the man who now hunted her as persistently as the cancer hunted Kara's young, helpless body.

The fantasies were her only saving grace. They made her feel alive. A feeling she craved even more than her next breath. Her neck still throbbed from the pressure of the gloved hands.

"Thank you," she murmured, throwing her arms around him, needing his strength to fuel her own the way it had only a few moments ago.

He stayed rigid for a long moment before he seemed to come to some decision. His arms slid around her, chasing away the cold as his heat surrounded her.

"It's okay."

It *was* okay because he was here. Comforting her. Touching her.

Yet it wasn't enough.

She leaned back and tilted her head up, staring into his eyes, seeing her own desire reflected in his gaze. For a split second, the hesitation that lived and breathed inside of her gripped her and held her immobile.

She'd been suppressing her needs and ignoring her own desire for so long that it had become habit. But then he moved his hands, his fingers sliding up the length of her spine, under her hair to cup her head, and her misgivings fled in a wave of longing that made her cry out.

He wanted to kiss her. She saw it in the bright light that lit his eyes as he stared at her, into her. The pulse in his neck jumped and his nostrils flared and his arms tightened, his fingers spreading through her hair in a grip that was so strong it was almost painful.

But he didn't hurt her. Funny, but despite who he was, what he was, she knew he wouldn't hurt her.

He'd saved her from her attacker.

From her nightmares.

From failure.

She'd sold her soul for success.

But while Cain had promised to help her succeed, he'd made no such agreement to chase away her nightmares. He didn't have to walk into her dreams and comfort her. All he was required to do was help with the experiments.

He did more because he wanted to. Because he desired her as must as she desired him.

Because he's an incubus. A sexual demon. He

wants sex. You are merely a warm body to supply him with his fix.

Make that a *hot* body. Very hot.

She was on fire, burning for his touch and aching for even more.

She closed her eyes and licked her lips in anticipation. It didn't matter why he wanted her, only that he did. And she wanted him. She knew how good he tasted, how hot and wet his kiss, how passionate, and suddenly she needed to feel all of those things.

She desperately needed to feel something besides the fear and the dread.

His breath brushed her lips and a tremor of need went through her. He was close. So very close . . .

"No."

The deep voice whispered through her head a split second before the warmth disappeared and the coldness closed in.

Sophie opened her eyes, leaving behind her dream in favor of reality. She lay in her bedroom where she'd fallen into a restless sleep earlier that evening, her thoughts haunted by the fear she'd felt on the way home, courtesy of her invisible stalker.

The sheets were twisted around her legs as if she'd been struggling, the pillows scattered across the carpet. A tree branch swayed with the wind outside her window and the shadows danced around her.

A nightmare, she assured herself once again.

She'd imagined everything. The pursuit, the struggle, the salvation.

She searched for the relief that usually came when she opened her eyes and realized that she'd been having a bad dream, but felt none.

There really was someone after her. Someone who'd gone so far as to break into her lab and follow her home.

Because of the formula?

Carol thought so and Sophie was inclined to agree. Someone wanted the formula and they would stop at nothing to get it.

You're jumping to conclusions.

Maybe.

While she'd dreamt the worst—that whoever it was wanted her dead—she could be over-reacting. Burglary and assault were very different crimes. And murder . . .

She refused to consider the option without more proof that whoever it was wanted to harm her directly. Right now, they'd merely rummaged around her lab and scared the daylights out of her.

Nothing more.

While she intended to be careful with her work and watch her back, she wasn't going to keep jumping at shadows and making more of a situation that hadn't yet escalated.

She would wait and watch and be careful.

As for Cain . . .

His hesitation had been part of her dream, as well. Crazy because he never held back in her dreams. Because they were *her* dreams. She used her own imagination based on her own needs. If he hadn't kissed her tonight, it had been because deep, down inside she hadn't really wanted him to.

Perhaps she'd been too afraid by the leather-covered fingers, or maybe she'd wanted merely a protector tonight rather than a lover.

She was the one who'd held back, not him.

Cain was the ultimate seducer. He gave new meaning to the word seduction with his smiles and his heated glances. He made work a constant push-pull between desire and duty. Sophie couldn't remember the last time she'd been able to truly concentrate at her lab. She was too aware of him and he was too much of a distraction with his touches and his kisses.

Like tonight *before* the dream.

If only he were to back off from his seductive techniques. Then she might be able to concentrate and forget her ridiculous infatuation with him.

She needed to forget because everything else was getting much too complicated. Her deadline loomed closer and danger lurked just around the corner with intentions she'd yet to figure out. She had enough to worry over without wondering when Cain was going to smile at her, or touch her, or kiss her, or more . . .

It was the *more* that had her so worked up. The anticipation of it. She was a healthy female. Of course she would be physically stimulated by a really hot man.

Make that a really hot incubus.

Especially an incubus. That was his job, so to speak. His duty when he wasn't using his special powers to help her uncover the final formula for *Forever Young*, and he was all the more distracting because of it.

But if he were to hold back all that seductive charm and give her some breathing room . . . ah, then she could think. Function. Focus.

She drew in a deep breath, her decision made.

First thing tomorrow evening, she was walking into the lab and telling him, point blank, to back off.

Or else.

He'd backed off.

Sophie watched him from her seat at the lab station. He stood clear across the room behind another counter, his gaze fixed on the three beakers in front of him. He extracted a small measurement of one powder and added it to a petrie dish. Then he cupped the petrie dish in his hands and closed his eyes as if completely oblivious to the fact that she watched him.

He'd been oblivious for three hours now.

She'd watched him for three hours.

Watched when she should have had her mind on the petrie dishes sitting in front of her. Cain had placed them there, each containing a certain measurement for her to test.

She shook her head and fixed her attention on the blue powder. With trembling hands, she retrieved her eyedropper and extracted the contents of the second petrie dish. Adding the compound, she stirred the powderlike crystals before dumping both ingredients into a beaker for heating.

Speaking of heat, she tugged at the collar of her blouse. With the butane burner fired on high only a few inches away from her, she was already sweating.

The heat certainly didn't come from Cain and his usually hot glances.

Not tonight.

They'd been working for over three hours and he'd barely said two words to her. He'd glanced at her even less, pausing only once to tell her to quiet down on her own experiments so that he could concentrate. And there'd been nothing but cold indifference in his gaze.

Nothing that would have made her sweat.

Except maybe the way he moved his fingertips around the rim of the petrie dish. He traced the edge before sliding his fingers underneath and cupping, holding . . .

The sight stirred her memory and she felt

those same hands on her bottom, cupping and holding and . . .

She blew out an exasperated breath, the sound louder than it should have been. He didn't so much as spare her a glance. Nothing.

He'd backed off, all right.

Thankfully.

So why didn't she feel so thankful?

She licked her lips and wiped at her sweat-lined brow. Hot. That's how she felt. And frustrated. Damned frustrated—

The thought ground to a halt as the mixture bubbled and popped and the chemical erupted over the edges of the beaker like a volcano.

She grabbed the container, moving it away from the flame and depositing it in a nearby sink filled with a stabilizing liquid.

"That wasn't supposed to happen," she said when she glanced up and found him staring at her as if she'd grown an eye in the middle of her forehead. "I mean, it was. I was just trying to see if there were any explosive properties to that particular mixture." *Right*. She'd goofed. Forgotten about the newly mixed compound and so now she had to start over.

All because of Cain.

Because she wanted him.

Whether he was teasing and tantalizing and trying to seduce her, or even when he was acting indifferent. She still wanted him and she finally admitted to herself that the longing wasn't going to go away until she did something about it.

Until she'd satisfied her curiosity and soothed her hormones once and for all.

The only way to truly focus was to get him out of her system. To go with the moment and enjoy the seduction. Then she could stop wondering and dreaming. She would truly know what it felt like to lie with him and make love. And the knowing was never quite as good as the anticipation.

That's what she needed. A good let-down. Then she could concentrate.

Speaking of concentration . . .

"I thought you said to stick with compounds A and B." She frowned at the fourth petrie dish he'd deposited on her desk a few moments ago. "This is neither."

"It's another stabilizing base. I thought we could mix it in and see what happens."

"But you said you were certain it was between A and B and that we just needed to determine the right amounts for each."

"I did say that, but now I'm thinking that we might want to test C. Just to be certain."

"But I thought you were—"

"Just mix in C and see what happens." He frowned and turned back to measuring various quantities, closing his eyes and touching each dish.

"Nothing's happening," she said after she'd

measured a standard amount of C and added it to A and B.

"Try a different amount."

"Introducing a new ingredient at this point is going to take even longer. It's a step backward."

"You want to find the answer, don't you?"

"More than anything," she said without hesitation.

Her reply drew his attention. His gaze locked with hers and he stared at her for a long moment. If she hadn't known better, she would have thought he was keeping something from her.

Right.

He was here to tell her everything he knew. He wanted to find the answer, otherwise his boss wouldn't get her soul.

No answer, no bargain, no reward.

"Why are you acting so funny?" she asked him.

"I am not acting funny. There is nothing humorous in this situation. I have not smiled once, have I?"

"I meant funny as in strange. Weird. What's up with you?"

"You ask too many questions."

"You don't have to be so grouchy."

"I am not grouchy."

"You're very grouchy." Kara's words echoed in her head and she couldn't help but smile. "Grouchy goat. That's what you are." She recited her goddaughter's favorite chant. "Grouchy goat, grouchy goat, grouchy goat—"

"Enough," he barked and her smile dissolved. "I'm trying to concentrate."

Fine. Two could play his game just as well as one. "So am I," she snapped. At least that's what she tried to do, but regardless of Cain's sudden indifference, she was anything but. Even across a room, she could feel his presence. Her skin prickled and her nostrils flared as she caught a whiff of the clean, masculine scent of him.

She couldn't help but wonder what it would feel like to touch him. *Really* touch him. And taste him. And make love to him.

Whew . . . it was definitely too hot in here.

She walked over to the thermostat on the wall and hiked the air conditioner down several notches. Cool relief blew from an overhead vent, but it did little to calm the fire that raged inside her.

With every moment that passed, Sophie became more convinced that the only real relief would be to get him off her mind by working him out of her system, and that meant satisfying her curiosity once and for all.

She needed to make love with him.

There would be no more wondering, daydreaming, fantasizing. They could actually spend their time thereafter working rather than lusting.

One night and she would finally have some perspective on things.

One, long, hot night.

It was the hottest night of Cain's afterlife.

A lofty statement considering he served the Devil himself. He'd stood in the very bowels of hell and still not been as flushed as he was at this very moment standing several feet away from Sophie Alexander.

Out of the corner of his eye, he watched her. She looked so soft and sweet and *wet*. Damp tendrils of dark hair hung loose from her ponytail, framing her face.

Perspiration dotted her forehead and beaded on her upper lip. Her lips glistened as she swiped them with her tongue before taking a long sip from the glass of cold water she'd retrieved from the water cooler.

"What I wouldn't give for some ice," she murmured. Her head snapped up a second later, as if to see if he'd heard her.

He quickly averted his gaze, focusing every ounce of attention on the containers in front of him.

When she seemed engrossed once again, he shifted his gaze back to her. He watched the slow trickle of a drop that had wound its way down her cheek, the graceful column of her neck to dip into the neckline of her blouse. He wanted so desperately to strip her naked and see where the moisture traveled. To watch the slow glide over her bare collarbone, the slope of her breast to puddle on the tip of one turgid nipple . . .

He forced the thought aside and concentrated on the petrie dish in his hand.

He closed his eyes, knowing even before he saw the vision of a useless experiment that the powder he held was in no way part of the final formula.

He knew, yet he still handed it to her a few minutes later for testing.

You're stalling, a voice whispered.

"Ridiculous," he muttered.

"What did you say?" Her voice floated from across the room and he realized that she'd heard him.

He gave her his most annoyed stare. "I said nothing."

"Yes, you did. I heard you."

"You did not."

"Yes, I did. You said—"

"There you go distracting me again," he growled. "Can a man have a moment's peace?"

"Bite me," she snapped before fixing her attention back on her work.

If only he could.

When the notion pushed into his head, he pushed it right back out. He could bite and suck and lick. He would do all of those things very soon.

Once he finished a thorough evaluation of all the possible ingredients. He had to be thorough. While he could rely on his visions, there was always the chance that he might be wrong.

An image of Sophie appeared in his mind. She sat crumpled on the floor, tears streaking her face, despair heavy on her heart, her eyes bright with pain.

Last night's vision.

He closed his eyes to the memory, desperate to block it out, to pretend that it didn't exist. That he'd never touched her hands and glimpsed her future.

There would be no future once she made the discovery. The bargain would be complete and her soul lost, and all because of him, because he was compelled to do the Evil One's bidding.

Because he enjoyed serving the dark lord himself.

He liked seducing woman after woman, and he would enjoy Sophie regardless of what waited for her.

The future was none of his concern. She was the one making the decision, dooming herself. He was merely answering her request.

Her decision.

So her tears shouldn't bother him, but damned if he could forget the sight of her moisture-streaked face, her eyes bright with anguish and pain and desperation.

He tried to force the thought aside. It was

none of his concern. He had no concern. He wasn't capable of such a feeling. Just lust.

Only and always the lust.

Aye, he felt that for her, all right.

More so than what he'd felt for any woman before. Because she wasn't just any woman. She was nothing like the women he'd encountered. They were all wrapped up in their own wants and needs. They bargained with the Devil on their own behalf.

But Sophie had sacrificed herself for none of the frivolous things he'd seen so many times in the past. She didn't seek eternal beauty or wealth. She'd sacrificed her soul for someone else, an act he couldn't help but admire.

If she only realized the consequences of her sacrifice. The pain. The suffering.

Then again, it would probably make no difference, and damned if that fact didn't stir even more admiration. A feeling that fed his desire even more than the voluptuous curves barely contained beneath her lab coat. His groin throbbed and his hands shook and his pulse bucked like a wild bull at a rodeo championship.

She'd sold her soul not for money or sex or any of the other things he'd seen over the years. She'd sacrificed herself, her eternity, for someone else.

Not that it mattered. Cain was obliged to

carry out his duty, which he fully intended to do.

Soon.

After he'd made certain that his instincts were correct and the exact ingredient amounts were just that—exact. He intended to leave nothing to chance.

At least that's what Cain told himself as the night wore on and he couldn't quite make himself hand her the exact ingredient amounts.

Instead, he had her performing useless experiments between three various ingredients, none of which would result in anything useful.

Still, he had to be sure. Sophie was a perfectionist and she expected conclusive results. That's what he intended to give her.

"This is ridiculous," she finally blurted after the clock struck midnight and her latest experiment erupted in a blur of purple smoke.

"Patience," he reminded her, shifting his gaze back to the petrie dish in his hand. "A good scientist must have patience." He held up the dish. "This could be it."

"And Brad Pitt's calling me later tonight for a date."

He set the dish aside. "A date?" What was she thinking? They were desperate to find a life-saving formula. "You do not have time for dating."

"It's a figure of speech. It's not going to happen. Only in my wildest dreams. Like this. This isn't going to happen tonight. I can feel it." She shrugged out of her labcoat. "I need to get out of here."

"You do look tired." What was he doing? He had no business encouraging her to call it quits. He didn't want her to call it quits because it meant that he couldn't complete his assignment.

No formula.

No seduction.

No eternal damnation.

The vision pushed its way into his head and he saw Sophie with the tears on her face, the pain bright in her eyes.

"I'm not tired. I'm frustrated. There's a big difference." There was no mistaking the meaning in her voice.

His gaze fixed on her bottom lip glistening from the quick swipe of her tongue. She'd shed her lab jacket thanks to the temperature in the room. Her nipples pressed against the fabric of her blouse, making mouthwatering indentations.

It was all Cain could do to shift his attention back to the petrie dish in his hand.

"Go home."

Now.

Before he changed his mind and did what he didn't want to do. For he couldn't touch her until she discovered the formula, and he wanted to touch her.

He needed it.

But he wouldn't.

Because of the deal, he told himself. He was bound by the agreement and so he had to follow the planned course of action.

No formula, no seduction.

The thought sent the usual ache through him, but for the first time, greater than his lust was the surge of protectiveness that welled inside him.

Protectiveness?

No, he had to be mistaken. He was merely being careful and following the rules.

He always followed the rules and now would be no different.

He couldn't let her condemn herself. Even in the name of love.

His reluctance to hand over the formula certainly had nothing to do with the fact that he couldn't stand the thought of letting her sacrifice herself for such an idealistic notion as love.

An action she would surely regret in the end just as he had. He'd sacrificed himself in the name of love, to avenge the only person other than his parents who'd truly loved him, and he'd regretted his decision.

The moment he'd felt the blood on his hands—regardless of the fact that it was his enemy's—he'd regretted his actions.

But it had been too late.

It wasn't too late for Sophie. Not yet.

She had time to change her mind. As long as the formula was incomplete, there was no bargain.

Not that that was the reason Cain held back. Caution guided him now. That was it.

At least that's what Cain kept telling himself, and perhaps in time, he might even believe it.

Chapter Twelve

A half hour after leaving the lab, Sophie was *still* burning up.

Despite the air-conditioned cab ride home.

She might as well have walked.

She hadn't because it wasn't nearly cool enough outside and she'd been eager to avoid a repeat of last night.

She'd done just that. Since saying goodbye to the extra ten security guards posted at various points throughout her office building, she'd walked straight out the door and into the nearest cab, and not once had the hair on her arms stood on end. Likewise, the ride home had been quiet and uneventful with the exception of the cab driver who'd screamed several colorful words at a pedestrian who'd crossed his path.

Maybe she *had* imagined last night.

That's what reason kept insisting, particularly since the police had found no prints except her own.

But she knew . . .

She forced her apprehension aside and stepped off the elevator onto her floor. With a quick glance either way, she started down the empty hallway. Everything was quiet much the way it had been at work. Most of the offices were locked up for the night with the exception of marketing, where Angela Marks had been burning the midnight oil to finish the commercial promo plans for a product Sophie had yet to perfect.

Two weeks and counting . . .

She had to *do* something.

At the thought, several options jumped into her mind, particularly one where she walked up to Cain, planted a big wet one on his lips and ripped all of his clothes off. Surely he wouldn't be indifferent then.

Then again, after the past few weeks of his smoldering glances and sexy smiles, tonight's standoffishness had come as a total surprise.

She'd expected him to take the initiative. One she'd had no intention of resisting this time.

Instead, he'd kept his distance and left her to wallow in her frustration.

Don't think about him, she told herself. *Just don't.*

She blew out an exasperated breath, slid the key into her apartment door, and turned the lock.

"You're sweating," Beth remarked as she glanced up from an open text book. "Is it that hot out there?"

It wasn't hot outside, it was hot inside. That was the trouble. Sophie's body temperature was raging and there was no relief in sight.

"It's not too bad. I'm just having hot flashes."

"Maybe you're getting close to the change." Beth closed the text book she'd been reading and started to gather up her notes.

"If only," Sophie muttered. She tugged at the collar of her blouse as she headed down the hall to peek in on Kara.

The little girl slept soundly, her small form flanked on the right by Tye Dye Barbie while the new Britney Spears doll lay on her left. On the floor lay an art pad surrounded by several drawings. Crayons scattered across the carpet.

The room was a mess and Sophie smiled anyway because Kara had made that mess, just like any other girl or boy her age.

"She was complaining about an upset stomach tonight," Beth whispered as she came up behind Sophie.

Sophie frowned and eyed her goddaughter. She noted her passive features and the faint shadowing beneath her eyes. "Any vomiting?"

"No. Just some cramping. At least that's what she described to me."

"Maybe she ate a little too much dinner." Sophie searched for a rational explanation, but her mind was already racing forward, her instincts on high alert as she mentally riffled through the list of symptoms for Kara's condition.

"That's what I was thinking. She *did* eat two Twinkies for dessert. I tried to stop her, but you know how that goes."

Sophie leaned down and touched her palm to Kara's forehead. Cool skin met hers and she let out a sigh of relief. She cast a knowing glance at Beth. "A flash of those blue eyes and you're putty in her hands."

"Actually, she threatened to call Calvin and tell him I've been listening to Willie Nelson."

"I thought you couldn't stand his music." Sophie left Kara's room and followed her sitter down the hall. That's when she noticed the slow, sweet harmony of *Blue Eyes Cryin' in the Rain* drifting from the stereo speakers.

"Well, he's no Enrique Iglesias, but he does have talent. You do have to admire his songwriting skills." Beth walked over and retrieved the CD from the player. "I also let her stay up a little past her bedtime. There was a Zsa Zsa Gabor tribute tonight—her birthday or something—and one of the cable stations was running back to back episodes of *Green Acres*.

216

I hope you don't mind. I know it was past her bedtime, but she's going to the hospital tomorrow for her check-up rather than school, so I figured it was okay."

"Rules are rules."

"That's what I told her. Then she threatened to tell him I not only am listening to Willie Nelson, but that I bought all of his CDs. Which isn't even true. I only bought four. The man's as old as God. He's got at least twenty out. Probably more. No way would I invest that much money in someone I barely like."

Sophie smiled. "It's okay. I know she can be stubborn." Besides, if she couldn't oblige Kara by moving right now, she could at least give her a glimpse of country living via television.

Until the real thing materialized, and it would.

Beth shoved the CD into her backpack, gathered up her things and said goodbye.

Sophie locked the door behind the girl, then headed for the bathroom and a cold shower. But even the icy spray didn't come close to dousing the fire that raged deep inside her.

Thanks to Cain.

"Forget him," she told herself yet again as she crawled into bed, a glass of ice water on the nightstand next to her.

She closed her eyes and tried to concentrate on something other than the way her nipples felt pressed against the soft cotton of her nightshirt. Or the way the sheets slid across her legs when she turned just so . . .

You're being watched, her sanity blurted, eager to distract her from the path her thoughts were taking. *Someone's watching and waiting. It could be Carol's ex, or it could be someone else. Maybe a competing company. Or maybe a stalker. Maybe someone who doesn't want your formula. Maybe he just wants you. Maybe he's been lusting after you from afar, eager to kiss you and touch you and—*

So much for a distraction.

She reached for the glass of ice by her bed and took a sip. There. That was better. Her mouth felt cool and hopefully the feeling would spread to the rest of her body. Just to be sure, she threw off the covers and peeled off her T-shirt. She needed all the air she could get.

Unfortunately, the sudden rush of air against her bare skin only heightened her senses. The breeze blew across her bare nipples and they hardened, pushing and begging for a lover they couldn't have. Cain had kept his distance tonight and she had no doubt that it would continue.

He'd looked so determined and stubborn and handsome.

She closed her eyes and saw him in her mind's eye. He stared back at her, his gaze bright with passion, his chest broad and bare and gleaming. He wore only a pair of blue jeans, the button undone. Right there in her mind's eye, the zipper slid down a fraction, revealing a thin line of dark blond hair that headed south.

The zipper slipped lower, lower, and Sophie found herself all the more mesmerized.

A dream, she knew. No way would he be teasing her, tempting her. Not the standoffish man she'd seen tonight. Yes, it was only a dream, but Sophie was frustrated and desperate and so she settled for the next best thing to the real Cain.

She reached for the fantasy.

This was a bad idea.

Cain stood in the bedroom doorway, his gaze fixed on Sophie as she lay stretched out on her bed. A very naked Sophie, except for the scrap of panties that barely covered the silky black triangle of hair at the base of her thighs. A few wisps peeked around the edges and his heart jammed in his throat.

He'd merely stepped through the shadows into her home to make sure she'd made it safely. After her nightmare last night, he, too, felt as if someone were after her. When he'd managed to turn his senses away from Sophie the night of the burglary, he'd been able to pick up on a presence. Someone had, indeed, been in her lab, despite what the authorities said.

Thankfully, she'd been cautious when she'd left tonight. She'd locked up all of her notes and computer disks, despite her hurry to get away from him.

He didn't blame her. He'd wanted some distance himself. Yet at the same time, he'd missed her after she'd left. And worried about her.

And so he was here.

His calm fled and every muscle in his body went on high alert as he drank in the sight of her. Her long, tanned legs. Her soft-looking thighs. Her scantily covered woman's mound. The dip of her belly button. The soft underside of her breasts. Rose-colored nipples hardened right before his eyes and his mouth watered.

One taste. That's all he needed. Just one and he could leash the beast that raged inside him.

But he couldn't chance it. No seduction until they discovered the formula, which they'd yet to accomplish.

Her dreams, a voice whispered. *Step into her dreams and prime her for the real thing*. He wanted to. Christ, how he wanted to but he wasn't so sure he could stop just shy of the real thing.

Not after last night's possession. She'd been too warm and tempting, her body welcoming him emotionally the way she would welcome him physically when he finally claimed her.

He couldn't risk getting that close to her, no matter how much he suddenly wanted to. A feeling that intensified when her eyelids fluttered open and she stared back at him, desire blatant in her gaze.

A dream, he reminded himself. She wasn't really awake or looking at him. This was her dream. She imagined seeing him there, beckoning to him, enticing him.

She sat up and reached for the glass of ice sitting on her nightstand. Fingering an ice cube, she touched the cold to her lips.

The reaction of her warm skin against the ice started a meltdown. Several drops of moisture slid from her mouth, down her chin and neck. She trailed the ice down her throat, over her collarbone, down the slope of one full breast.

A gasp parted her lips when she touched the ice to one nipple. The sound vibrated through him and he throbbed all the more fiercely. It was all he could do not to step forward. To take the ice in his own hands and run it over her blazing hot skin. To follow the path with his lips and his tongue.

"I'm so hot," she whispered. "I really need you, Cain. You're the only one who can cool me down. Please come over here. Please help."

But he didn't. For the first time in one of her dreams, he stepped back and forced himself to turn away.

He didn't trust his own control. Sophie affected him like no other and so he wasn't so sure he could abstain this time.

Better to keep his distance until after they'd uncovered the formula.

Until then, Sophie was strictly off limits.

"You're stalling." The Evil One's voice echoed in the blackness where Cain drifted a moment before a flame flickered and flared. The light blinded him and he blinked several times before he found his focus. He watched as the shadows pushed back, giving way to a circle of fire that surrounded the Evil One himself.

He looked truly evil tonight with his long, flowing black robe. The angles of his face were sharper than usual, his nose more hawked, his lips a razor-sharp line that hinted at his displeasure. His mirrorlike eyes reflected the orange flames and gave him an even more eerie air.

Cain shrugged off the fear that stirred in his belly. Not fear of the Evil One himself, but of the blackness surrounding them. Endless and absolute should the Evil One wish it upon Cain.

"It's going a little slower than I expected," he told the devil. "I just need time."

"I'm not a patient man."

"You're not a man," Cain pointed out.

The Evil One's eyes fired brighter and he held up one hand, revealing long, bony fingers tipped with razor-sharp claws. "Ah, for a moment I thought you had forgotten. You wouldn't forget such a thing, would you, Cain? You wouldn't forget the power that I wield? Or that I dictate your destiny?" He didn't wait for a reply. Instead, he reached through the flames.

Cain wanted to pull back, to lift a hand to defend himself, but he could do nothing for the Evil One held his soul. Paralyzed, he could only watch as one nail touched his shoulder and sliced through with agonizing slowness.

As always, his spirit mimicked the physical body he'd once possessed. His skin gaped open. Blood beaded and trickled from the wound. Pain bolted through Cain, consuming his senses and blinding him for several frantic heartbeats.

"Do not play me, Cain, for I am a much better player than you are. I do not like to be disobeyed."

"I'm almost there," he ground out, his teeth clenched, the agony in his shoulder making every breath a struggle. I just need a little time. We've got more experiments to run. To be sure." He ignored the voice that whispered that he was, indeed, stalling.

That he was fighting to give Sophie time to see the error of her ways, so that she would back out of the bargain before it was complete and the vision would be null and void.

He was doing no such thing. He merely wanted to be certain. He had to be certain for the outcome was too serious for mistakes.

"Time is almost up, dear boy." Another swipe

and Cain doubled over. "Do it soon. Or else you'll know a thousand times more pain and suffering."

The words thundered through his head followed by a roar of laughter that quickly faded to a still quiet.

The flames died down and Cain found himself locked in the blackness once again with only the damned visions for company.

Oddly enough, it wasn't past visions that haunted him now. It was a vision of Sophie's future.

As Cain watched the scene unfold yet again, he not only saw her pain, he felt it, and the feeling was worse than anything he'd ever felt at the hands of the Evil One.

For this wasn't his own suffering, but that of the woman he loved.

"She looks good, doesn't she?" Sophie smiled the next morning as she watched Kara through the two-way observation mirror in the pediatric unit of Chicago Memorial Hospital.

The little girl sat at a small table cluttered with toys. She rummaged here and there before retrieving a Barbie doll from the stack.

"She's still pale." Dr. Stevens jotted down a few notes on a pad before sliding the pen and paper into his lab coat pocket. He pushed his glasses up onto his nose and folded his arms, his gaze still hooked on Kara. "She looks tired."

"She stayed up late watching a *Green Acres* marathon on cable." At his questioning glance, she added, "It's her favorite sitcom. She wants to move to the country and get a pet pig."

"That's out of the question."

"I know it's not a possibility right at this moment, but I'm hoping—"

"It's ridiculous, Sophie. Be realistic. She's a very sick girl. She has to be near state-of-the-art medical care. Do you know how rare her condition is? This type of cancer affects one in a million. There are very few facilities that can deal with this." He shook his head. "She has to be here. I've been working on a new program to treat just this type of disease. If it works, it will be groundbreaking and Kara is a prime candidate if we start now."

"Not if it involves more chemo."

"It's a new and improved form of chemotherapy. It uses the latest in laser radiation therapy."

"It's still chemo." She shook her head. "If she gets sick again, we'll do it. But not until then."

"There is no *if*. Don't you understand that? It's simply a matter of when."

"Maybe."

"We're close, Sophie. Very close."

Cain's words played through her head and she smiled because he was right. They *were* close. The formula was right there and it was only a matter of time.

And they had time. Kara looked good. She had pink cheeks and a wide smile and she was still in remission. Last night's tummy episode had merely been the result of too much junk food.

"If we wait until it's necessary, it will be too late. This therapy is extreme. It's too taxing to be undertaken when the patient is ill. It has to start while the body is healthy, so that it can endure the treatment. If she's too sick, it will be too late. Are you willing to risk that?"

Sure-shot Stevens. Sophie remembered his reputation and fear stirred deep inside her. A feeling she quickly pushed aside. *Not this time.*

"I'm not risking anything because she's going to be okay."

"You seem very confident."

"I am."

"I wish I could be as sure, but I'm afraid I've seen too many cases like this end in disaster. An end that doesn't have to come if you'll just agree to this treatment right now while she's strong enough to withstand it."

"Physically, maybe. But emotionally . . . I'd rather wait on a different solution. A more permanent one with a better success rate."

"You've made some progress, haven't you?"

"Some." She smiled. "A lot. I really think this is it."

"I would like to be the judge of that."

"You will be. When I have something solid,

then I'll hand things over to you and your team and you can take it from there."

"I prefer to work during the developmental stage."

"Thanks, but I can do it myself."

"I hope you're right. I wouldn't want Kara to pay the price for your mistake."

"She won't," Sophie said, the words filled with a determination that was becoming harder and harder to maintain in the face of Dr. Stevens's pessimism.

Realism, she reminded herself. He was a realist and so she couldn't blame him for his doubt.

"I know you're just trying to be helpful, but I'm doing what I feel is best right now. Please understand that. As her physician, her care is my top priority. If you refuse that care, that's your business."

"I'm not refusing care. I just don't think that she needs more chemo at this point."

"It's not your typical chemotherapy."

"Does it have side effects?"

He didn't answer. "Everything has side effects."

"Are they typical of regular chemo treatments?" When he didn't answer, she went on, "I won't agree right now. She feels good. Normal. For the first time in a long time. That's the way I want things to stay. The way they *will* stay."

227

"With a little pain now, perhaps she can feel better for the future."

"There's a different way."

"I know you're an expert in your field, Sophie, but this is medicine we're talking about. If there were a different way, don't you think I would know? This is my area of expertise." He shook his head. "This is the only answer, and it's not that bad of one. I've seen children undergo this treatment. It's risky, but it has a high success rate for prolonging life at least two to five years."

"I want twenty to fifty years. Can you guarantee me that?" When he didn't answer, she shook her head. "Kara's not a statistic. She's a little girl and she wants to move to the country. We've got a place in Gruene that her family left. That's her dream. Our dream. I want her to see it realized."

"After the treatment, you can visit—"

"She wants to live there. To *live*. Not wait for the next batch of treatments or wither away from what's eating her from the inside out. *Live*, Dr. Stevens. Your treatment can prolong the way she is now. For a little while. I want to make the remission permanent. I want to stop the cancer for good, and I will." She turned toward Kara. "I will."

"I'm still going to recommend her for the program. A research team will take it from there and contact you for background information. We might as well start the preliminary process, that way when things don't work out, she's ready to start as soon as possible."

She wanted to shake her head, but one glance at Kara and she realized that she had to be realistic, as well. She nodded. "We'll do the preliminaries, so *if* things don't work out we're ready to go."

He frowned at her for a long moment before nodding. "Fair enough."

"But it's Friday night," Kara whined later that evening, after a full day of various testing at the hospital. "You've been working all week and I haven't hardly seen you. Can't you just take tonight off? Just once? Please." Kara accented the plea by grabbing Sophie around the waist and holding tight. "We can order pizza and draw pictures and make root beer floats and watch *The Beverly Hillbillies.*"

"What about *Green Acres?*"

"That was last night. Tonight there doing a Jethro and Ellie May marathon. They moved to the city, but Granny wants to go back home. I don't blame her. I don't like the cement pond. Ponds are supposed to have mud on the bottom and grass surrounding them and fish swimming inside. A cement pond is unnatural."

"Unnatural, huh?"

"That's the new word for the day. I picked it out of the dictionary and Beth read it to me. She said it was a really good word to pick. She also said that her boyfriend has this unnatural fat fish for Willie Nelson." Kara looked puzzled. "Are fish not supposed to be fat? 'Cause I've seen whales and they're kind of fat."

"I think she meant fetish. A fetish is when you really *really* like something."

"I have a fetish for pizza."

"Exactly."

"And you have a fetish for work."

"I have a responsibility to provide for us, that's why I work."

"I think Beth has a fetish for Jethro because when she found out that it was marathon night, she said that she wouldn't mind kicking back with some pizza and watching because she thinks Jethro is really cute for a country boy." Kara shrugged. "Actually, I think Duke is cuter. He's the hound dog. Maybe we could have a hound dog."

"I thought you wanted two pigs?"

"A hound dog and two pigs. And maybe a few chickens. If you live in the country, you *have* to have chickens. Or it's just unnatural." She smiled up at Sophie. "So can you stay home tonight? Please." She frowned. "When I grow up I'm never going to work."

"You have to work. To take care of yourself and your family. Because you love them."

"But if I work, then they won't know how much I love them because I'll be too busy working to show them I love them."

"How old are you?"

"Six and a half." She smiled. "You know that."

"For a second I thought you were twenty-eight."

"You're twenty-eight."

"Then I should be the one making all the sense, shouldn't I?"

"I don't understand."

"Nevermind." Sophie shook her head and reached for the phone. "Pepperoni or hamburger?"

"Both."

"Both it is. Why don't you go get the art tablet and colors." She watched Kara head for her bedroom before dialing the number for Pino's Pizza Palace. While she needed to work, she also needed to take the time to remember what she was working so hard for. One night wasn't going to make that much of a difference, particularly since she hadn't been getting anywhere due to lack of concentration.

Thanks to Cain.

An image from last night's dream pushed into her head and she saw him so tall and strong, his body perfectly sculpted, standing in the moonlight, his gaze hungry as he watched her glide the ice over her skin.

A burst of longing went through her and she groaned.

"What's wrong, Aunt Sophie?" Kara called from her room. "You sound funny."

"Nothing. Just trying to decide if we want extra cheese."

"We *have* to have extra cheese."

"Extra cheese it is." But even more than a rush of fattening pizza, Sophie needed something *really* gratifying.

"I think I've got Oreos in the kitchen," she said as Kara walked back into the living room, her arms overflowing with art supplies. "Are you up to some Oreos?" Nothing like chocolate to kill a craving.

Another image of Cain pushed into her head and she saw him hard and naked and wet, thanks to the ice she'd wanted desperately to use on his sculpted body.

Her stomach rumbled and her thighs quivered. "Forget the Oreos. Let's head down to the Marble Slab for a scoop of double chocolate brownie bomb." Sure it was a quick fix, but a girl had to do what a girl had to do.

Where in the hell was she?

Cain paced the length of her laboratory and glanced at the clock for the umpteenth time. She was late. Hours late.

Another minute ticked by and the numbers rolled and his patience level reached the limit.

It was midnight and she still wasn't here.

Something was wrong.

The notion sent him racing for the shadows in the far corner. He stepped forward and the darkness embraced him for several long moments before he took another step and found himself in her apartment.

The drapes were drawn, the only light coming from the television set. Colorful images danced across the screen, casting a multicolored glow on the woman and child that lay on opposite ends of the couch.

Relief washed through him as he noted the steady rise and fall of Sophie's chest. One arm dangled over the side of the couch. The other held the feet of the child that lay opposite her.

She was all right.

Alive.

Relief fled as reality settled in. She'd stood him up on purpose.

He marched across the living room, ready to grab her by the shoulders and shake some manners into her. He'd been worried sick about her. Anything could have happened. Her nightmare could have materialized—

"Who are you?" The soft voice sent his thoughts careening to a stop. He halted just an inch shy of actually touching Sophie. His hand fell away as his gaze shifted to the little girl. Bright blue eyes stared back at him. "Can't you talk?"

"W—what?"

"You can talk." She smiled, seemingly pleased at the discovery.

Not afraid or weary or any of the other reactions a demon would normally expect.

Then again, he wasn't a typical demon. He looked human. He felt human. Especially at this moment during the witching hour.

"Of course I can talk," he replied.

"So what's your name?"

"Cain."

"I'm Kara." She smiled again and something shifted in his chest. It had been a long time since a child had smiled at him. He'd never had children of his own. His wife had been killed before giving birth. All of the children in the village had feared him or been in awe. None had ever smiled at him even when he'd been a child himself.

He'd been shunned, looked upon as evil. Or worse, feared.

"You're an angel, aren't you?"

A dark angel, but he didn't tell her that. For some reason, he didn't want her to be afraid of him. "Sort of."

"You look like an angel."

She seemed so sure and he couldn't help but smile himself. "And how would you know, little one, what an angel looks like?"

"Because I've seen one." Her eyes grew wider, her face more somber. "She's beautiful, like a princess, and she's helping me. She's my guardian angel. I bet you're Aunt Sophie's guardian angel."

"I am here to help her, yes." *Then condemn her*, his conscience whispered.

Crazy, considering he wasn't supposed to have one. Then again, he wasn't supposed to feel compassion or sympathy or regret or remorse or any of the things he felt when he was with Sophie.

Least of all love.

"You should go back to sleep." He forced the notion aside and tried to turn his attention to Sophie.

But there was just something about the child's eyes that kept him from looking away. It wasn't so much their color or shape, but the emotions blazing deep in their depths. She looked at him with such trust and compassion and . . . hope.

As if he really were a guardian angel.

In reality, he was the angel of death as long as he stood between Sophie and her formula. For Kara would surely die if the discovery failed.

She smiled at him and in a crystalline moment, he understood why Sophie would risk everything for this small child. Because she *was* a child.

Innocent.

Pure.

Untainted by the evil of the world, despite her illness.

She still held her optimism, her faith in human nature. She hadn't been spoiled the way he'd been so long ago when the village had shunned and feared him. She still looked at the world as a special place to be.

She deserved a chance at life because she was life. She was everything good and special.

She was the sun smiling in bright yellow crayon from a nearby drawing.

"You like that?" She reached over and grabbed the picture. "You can have it."

He stared down at the drawing, his eyes burning.

Crazy. It was just a picture. A child's scribble. It wasn't real, yet it warmed him as if he'd been gazing at the sun itself.

"Help her, okay?" The soft voice drew his attention again. "She needs help right now. She's tired." She yawned. "And so am I. I haven't been feeling very good lately, but I haven't said anything. She'll worry and I don't want her to. I want everything to be okay so that we can move away from here to the country. Have you ever been to the country?" Before he could answer her question, she smiled. "Of course you have. You've been everywhere." She rubbed her stomach and made a face. "I really don't feel so good."

"It's okay—" he started, reaching out. His fingers froze a hairsbreadth shy, stopped by an invisible force.

He couldn't touch her because she was an innocent and he was tainted.

Evil.

The truth rang through him the way it had his entire life and afterlife. Oddly enough, he didn't feel the usual bitterness. Instead, he felt a deep sadness for all those who'd feared him. He realized that it hadn't been their fault. People feared what they didn't understand and they reacted accordingly.

But he wasn't truly evil. Evil was something created. A harmful act or a mean word. It wasn't inborn. Goodness was the essence of man and he saw that in Kara.

In her smile.

In her optimism despite the evil gnawing away at her courage.

He gripped the edge of the blanket and spread it over her.

"Thank you," she said, "and thank you for helping Aunt Sophie."

But Cain was the one who wanted to say thank you for this little girl had given him something very precious. She'd given him a sun as brilliant as the one he so desperately missed, and with just a trusting glance and a genuine smile, she'd given him peace with his past.

And for that, he owed her.

Chapter Thirteen

"That snake-in-the-grass is right under our noses. I can just feel it." Carol, as professional as ever in a pale pink jacket and skirt, paced in front of Sophie's desk the next afternoon. "But if he expects me to just give up without a fight, he's got another thing coming." She handed Sophie a list of new security codes. "We're changing *daily*."

"What happened to once a week?"

"A burglary, that's what happened. I don't care what the police say. Jeffrey was in here. He knows you're close, Sophie. Speaking of which, how close are you?"

"A few days. A week at the most," she said, her fingers crossed that she wasn't telling a lie.

"We'd better hurry along. The pageant is next

week." She smiled. "I know all this stress is probably making you crazy, but just try to relax and keep working. I've got the best security specialist in Chicago working for me now. He'll make sure this place is locked up tighter than Jeffrey's stupid alibi for the night of the break-in. Whatever you need," she pointed to the suited gentleman standing by the door, "just let Jake know. He's your personal bodyguard for the evening."

"I really don't need—"

"You, your work and this lab. Someone will be stationed right outside your doorway twenty-four/seven. If anyone tries to get in or out of here, we'll catch them—"

"Hey, watch the suit, will ya?" Angela Marks pushed at the large hands that shot out to bar her entrance into Sophie's lab. "I work here, all right?"

"Sorry, but this area is off-limits to everyone," the man told her.

"It's okay, Jake," Carol said, waving to the security officer. "The only thing you have to fear from Angela is losing your donut if your not fast enough getting to the pastry cart in the morning."

"What can I say?" Angela shrugged. "I've got a Krispy Kreme fetish." She plopped down on the corner of Sophie's desk and crossed her stocking-clad legs. "How are you doing?"

Sophie leaned back and eyed Angela who

loomed ever closer. "Fine. Thanks for asking."

"Don't get all girlie on me. I'm not talking about you personally even though I hear you had the crap scared out of you the other night. I've got four commercial spots ready to go for the new product. I need a new product."

"Don't we all," Carol said.

"So? What's going on with it? Is it going to be ready by Monday?"

"Hopefully."

"I'd rather hear something a little more definite, like *yes*."

"Yes, I hope it will be ready by Monday."

"It will be," Carol said with confidence. "And everything will be okay. It will be."

"You been watching those positive mantra videos again?" Angela arched an eyebrow. It was common knowledge that Carol had a self-help addiction. Since the divorce, she'd gone on a huge self-improvement kick. She'd had liposuction, rhinoplasty and breast implants. She'd also gone on to learn everything from Spanish to French pastry cooking. While the job kept her too busy for classes and seminars these days, she was always ordering new videos via the Internet. She'd amassed a collection that included everything from Improving Your Posture in Ten Days to Breathing Techniques for Business Executives.

"Actually, I've been watching Madame Tobey's Do It Yourself Voodoo Curses. I acciden-

tally logged onto her site when I was re-
searching new veal recipes. I've always wanted
to learn how to prepare veal. Anyhow, the positive mantra thing I taped on Dr. Phil last week.

Now," Carol blew out a deep, even breath,
"I've got a business dinner to go to, so back to
work," she motioned to Sophie, "You've got a
deadline to make."

"Amen to that," Angela said. "I know you've
got it narrowed down to two compounds, but
you're still a ways off."

"How did you know I've got it narrowed down
to two?"

"Carol told me. Your last update to her."

"Oh." The thing was, Sophie didn't remember
mentioning a specific number in her last update. She'd said narrowed down, but she hadn't
said how many substances. Had she?

She made a mental note to pull up her copy
of the report and take a look.

In the meantime . . .

"If you'll excuse me," she told Angela, reaching for the petrie dish the woman had just
picked up. "You really shouldn't touch the active ingredients. It could be dangerous."

"Sure thing." She slid off the edge of the
counter. "I'm down the hall if you want to
buddy up later when you leave. It's kind of scary
leaving here by yourself. Who knows what
could be lurking in the shadows." She winked

and a strange sense of awareness swept through Sophie.

The feeling that something wasn't quite right and that Angela was a part of it rooted inside her.

He's right under our noses. Carol's words echoed back to her and she remembered her own misgivings about the marketing executive. Angela was always working late, always hanging around.

Maybe.

And maybe she was looking for a scapegoat. A face to go with the threat so that it didn't seem as surreal. Better to know your enemies than fear the unknown.

If Angela were working for Jeffrey, then he would have a definite inside track. Angela had full security clearance and while she didn't have access to Sophie's lab—no one other than Sophie and Carol and business security had that clearance—she could nosey around, ask questions, and get the initial scoop once the formula was perfected. She controlled the media. She could leak the product information *before* the public was made aware.

Sophie drew in a deep breath. Angela was the least of her problems at this point. She needed a final formula and until then, she would merely be cautious and keep her eyes open for anything out of the ordinary.

She couldn't let her imagination get the best

of her. She had to stay focused on the here and now.

She drew the blinds, blocking out the last of the sun's rays. The room plunged into shadows. Sophie was just an arm's length shy of the lamp when she heard Cain's voice.

"There's no reason to be afraid."

"I'm not afraid." She flipped on the light and turned to face him.

He stood a few feet away, his arms folded as he leaned against the wall and observed her.

"You could have fooled me. You look frightened." Concern glittered in his eyes and a warmth spread through her.

Heat.

That's what he should make her feel. Just lots of breath-stealing heat.

Not *warm*.

Warm was something she felt when she played with Snowball or watched Kara at the park. *Warm* was a feeling associated with genuine affection. With liking someone. With loving them.

As soon as the thought rooted in her mind, she tried to push it back out and couldn't.

"You don't have to be fearful of anyone. I'm here."

The words were meant to comfort and damned if they didn't do just that. She grew warmer, feeling content and *safe*, of all things.

Crazy. She was supposed to feel hot and bothered and off balance when he was near. Now she felt all of those things and more.

Too much more.

Feelings he obviously didn't share. Of course he seemed concerned about her well-being. He needed her safe until the formula was discovered and the bargain complete. Otherwise, he wouldn't get her soul for his boss.

Even as the truth echoed through her head, denial niggled inside her. She couldn't forget the pain she'd seen in his eyes when he'd mentioned his past to her, the desperation she'd seen on his face, as if he'd wanted to know love as badly as she had as a child. The disappointment because he'd never had anyone to depend on any more than she'd had. Most of all, she couldn't forget the warmth she'd seen in his eyes when he'd saved her in the dream or the possessiveness she'd felt in his touch as he'd reached out and embraced her.

Just a dream, she told herself.

Make-believe.

Wishful thinking.

This was reality. The cold, aloof man—make that demon—standing before her.

For several frantic heartbeats, she was struck by the sheer masculine perfection of him. He wore jeans and a black T-shirt and black biker boots. The soft cotton of his shirt molded to his broad shoulders and heavily muscled biceps. Denim clung to his trim hips and sinewy thighs like a second skin. He was tall and big and powerful, exuding a magnetism that had undoubtedly drawn many a woman.

Sophie was no exception. At that moment, she couldn't look away. She could only look.

His eyes were a darker shade of green than usual, like a thick forest that blocked even the thinnest ray of sunlight. His hair hung loose and flowing, giving his already sharp features a dangerous air. His lips were a tad full for a man.

Sexy.

Mesmerizing.

No, she couldn't look away, but he could.

He did.

"We have to get to work," he said as he pushed away from the wall and started for the lab station set up on the opposite side of the room.

The command jarred her out of her thoughts and she swallowed against the longing that rose inside her.

As much as she wanted him, he didn't want her. He'd made that clear with his standoffishness and while she was half-tempted to throw herself into his arms and blurt out the thoughts racing through her head, she wouldn't.

Old habits died hard and Sophie had been taking the defensive, rejecting those who'd rejected her for much too long to change her ways now.

245

If he wanted distance, she would oblige him. After all, she had work to do.

"This is it." Sophie stared into the microscope and added a drop of the accelerated growth compound she'd used to test every possible combination to date. Usually, the compound would mingle in with the damaged cells and start working its destruction, tearing down the structure and destroying each cell within a matter of minutes.

Not this time.

The clock ticked away as she stared through the microscope, her heart pounding faster and faster. The damaged cells she'd treated with the stabilizer Cain had handed her over an hour ago remained completely unaffected, their initial state preserved.

One hour and counting . . .

She smiled at him. "We've got it. This time, I really think we've got it. It's been an hour and nothing's changed. The damaged cells are still in their original state. An *hour*." Her excited gaze shifted to his. "This could really be it."

"This *is* it." Cain pushed up from the chair where he'd been sitting and watching since handing her the petrie dish with the exact ingredient amounts.

He walked around the desk and paced the length of the room, his boots clicking with each footstep. "This is what you've been waiting for. This is *Forever Young.*"

She took another look into the microscope, noted the continued preservation. Her smile widened.

"Just like that." She shook her head. "Yesterday we were still testing out in left field and now . . . I can't believe it." She let out a deep breath and tried to calm her stampeding heart. It was too much. All that work and now it was here, right in front of her, just like that.

It was too good to be true.

The thought rooted in her head and skepticism crept in. Her smile faded as she forced a deep breath and reached for another slide. There were a battery of tests to be run in order to be certain. Results to document. Charts that had to be completed before any conclusions could be made. A scientific process to follow, and Sophie was, after all, a scientist.

She wouldn't draw any conclusions until the last experiment had been documented and her theory proven beyond a doubt.

"You don't have to do that," Cain told her as she started to subject another slide to the compound.

"Yes, I do. I have to be sure."

"I am sure."

"I'm not." She leaned down and peered into the microscope. "Not yet."

*   *   *

"This *is* it." She leaned back in her chair and let loose a loud whoop.

No sooner had the noise exploded than the doorknob turned. Jake appeared, gun drawn. His frantic gaze spanned the room before coming to rest on Sophie.

"Is everything all right, ma'am?"

"Everything is perfect." She beamed. "I didn't meant to cause a stir, but my experiment went well."

"Oh." He scanned the room again, as if not quite believing her, before nodding. "Call out if you need anything." The door shut and Sophie turned, fully expecting Cain to be standing behind her.

Instead, he was gone.

Shadows crowded the far corner of the room where the light didn't quite reach. But she could see well enough to know that no one was there.

He'd left.

She tried to hide her sudden disappointment and concentrate on her discovery.

The formula.

The *final* formula.

"I did it," she told Dr. Stevens several minutes later after going through his emergency paging system.

"What are you talking about?"

"A youth formula," she rushed on. "I've got a stabilizing compound that actually works. It will hold damaged cells in their existing state with no degeneration."

"There's no such thing."

"There wasn't until about an hour ago." She packed away the last of the experiment findings into one of the cabinets, turned the lock and deposited the key into her pocket. "Can we meet tomorrow morning? I want you to see this, then you and your team can take it from there and come up with a viable treatment plan."

"I think you're getting ahead of yourself. Let's say for argument's sake, that you're on to something. It could take years to develop and—"

"It won't take years. Once you see my research, you'll know that. It works on skin cells which have the same composition as organ cells. It works."

"I know it may seem that way now but—"

"Just meet with me and see for yourself."

"I've got a meeting at nine in the morning."

"We can do it afterwards."

"No good. I've got to be at the hospital. I could squeeze you in at, say . . . seven thirty at my office?"

"I'll be there."

Sophie entered the final documentation on her notes and tried to ignore the strange niggling that something was wrong.

Something *was* wrong. She'd made the discovery of a lifetime and she was alone. She needed to celebrate. But first . . .

She backed up her computer notes and slipped the backup diskette into her lab coat before locking everything up in her file cabinet.

"See you tomorrow, Jake," she said as she left the room and headed down the hall.

As excited as she was, she was also nervous on the way home. But not too nervous to risk a stop by the grocery store for a few pints of celebratory ice cream.

"She's asleep," Beth told her when she walked in the door a little after ten o'clock. "I think she played too hard."

That's what Sophie wanted to think, but when she glanced in on Kara, she couldn't help but note the dark circles under her eyes. Her first instinct was to shake the little girl just to make sure she was okay. To see Kara smile and hear her words of reassurance.

You're jumping the gun. She's just tired.

Sophie held tight to the knowledge and forced herself to calm down. She was overly worried when she should be excited. Joyous. Ecstatic.

Nervous.

The deal was complete, but she'd yet to turn over her information to Dr. Stevens. What if she didn't make tomorrow's meeting?

She remembered the feel of the gloved hands at her throat, choking the life out of her and she shivered.

"Are you okay?" Beth asked as she gathered up her things in the living room.

"Fine, but I'd be better if you would do a favor for me." She pulled the diskette from her lab pocket. "Hold on to this and if anything happens to me . . ."

Beth stared at her as if she'd grown two heads.

"I know it sounds funny, but just listen. I need you to hold on to this and if anything happens to me—if I mysteriously die in my sleep or get hit by a bolt of lightning or something—make sure you give it to Dr. Stevens. He'll know what it's about."

"You're wigging me out a little. I mean, the sky's clear and no rain's even predicted. Lightning is a pretty off-the-wall concept at this point."

"My lab was burglarized and I have reason to think someone is after my work, which means they will go through me to get to it."

"Right."

"Carol Peterson thinks it's a corporate conspiracy and I'm likely to agree. It's the only answer I can come up with."

"You're serious, aren't you?"

"As a heart attack, speaking of which, if that happens, then you're to follow through to Dr. Stevens." At Beth incredulous expression, Sophie added, "I'm sure I'll be fine, but I can't risk not getting this information to Dr. Stevens. It's for Kara, which is why I need a backup plan just in case."

"And I'm the backup."

"If you'll agree."

"If anything happens to you, I go to Dr. Stevens with this." She fingered the diskette.

"Exactly." When Beth started to ask another question, Sophie held up her hand. "Don't. Just trust me and do as I ask. Please."

She hesitated a moment before finally nodding and packing the diskette into her book bag. "Whatever you say. Look, I've got a date tonight, but I could cancel. I mean, Calvin and I are just going to sit around listening to the best of Willie, which I've heard before. So if you want someone to stay over—"

"Go. I'm fine." She held up a pint of ice cream. "I've got a date, too."

Beth looked hesitant, but she finally nodded.

A few minutes later, Sophie locked the door behind her sitter, then headed back into the living room after retrieving a pint of ice cream and a spoon and settled down on the sofa. A quick scan through the TV programs and she opted to just shut the contraption off to stare at the stars twinkling just beyond the open window.

Chocolate exploded on her tongue with the first bite, but it didn't fill her with the usual rush.

"No more chemotherapy," she reminded herself, reaching for the joy she'd felt at the initial discovery. "No more experimental drugs or self-righteous specialists with their dismal prognosis. No more."

She pushed to her feet and walked to the large bay window. Staring out, she fixed her attention on one of the stars in the far distance. That's what she felt like. That one star so far removed from all the others.

Alone.

Lonely.

The way she'd felt most of her life.

The way Cain had felt most of his life.

As if her thoughts had conjured him, she caught his reflection in the window next to her and turned.

"You left before I had a chance to thank you." The reality of what she'd done tonight crystalized and her eyes suddenly filled with tears.

She turned back to the window and rested her forehead against the cool glass. Moisture slid from her eyes, gliding down her face to drip-drop onto her hands.

"Sophie." Cain's deep voice preceded the strong touch on her shoulder. "Don't cry. Please."

"I'm sorry. I just . . ." She shook her head. "I mean, I tried so hard to convince myself that I would find it, but I didn't really believe it. But now . . . It's done." She opened her eyes and stared at him. "Thanks to you. You did it."

" 'Twas your work. Your vision. I merely helped things along."

"I wouldn't have made the discovery in time without you. Kara's still in remission. Geez, the pageant's not even here. There's still time to get the cream into development and get the promo spots done." The enormity of the discovery weighed down on her. "You not only saved my sweet Kara, but you saved me professionally, as well. You saved the entire company. I need to call Carol." She rested her hand atop the strong fingers gripping her shoulder. He went rigid beneath her touch, but it didn't put her off. She was too happy. Too indebted. "Thank you."

"Forget it." He shrugged away, pulling his hand from beneath hers. " 'Twas part of the deal."

"Deal or no deal, I'm thankful. This is all I've dreamt about for a very long time." She sniffled and wiped at her watery eyes. "You gave it to me. You're responsible—"

"No," he growled. "I did nothing. You did this. You bargained for an answer and so you have it." He paced the length of the room and she couldn't help herself.

She reached out for him, her hand resting atop his arm. Warm skin met her fingertips and she felt the turmoil that raged inside of him. The guilt. She saw it in the dark green depths of his eyes, heard it in the raw, husky quality of his voice.

"It was your choice."

"That's right. Mine and mine alone."

He shrugged away from her, walking to the far end of the living room where another window overlooked the street below. "I didn't call you. You called the Evil One. You made the deal," he reminded her, as if saying the words could convince himself.

"That's right."

"You *wanted* this. You asked for it."

"And I would do it again in a heartbeat."

His head whipped around and he stared at her, disbelief raging in his eyes. "You say that, but you don't know yet. You don't know how it feels."

Ah, but she did. She felt the strange tightening in her chest, as if invisible fingers reached inside and settled around her heart.

Her soul.

"It gets worse," he said, as if reading her thoughts, as if feeling the pain. "It gets much worse."

Her gaze hooked on the drawings scattered atop the coffee table. More of Kara's artwork.

Despite the pressure in her chest, she smiled. "I'm sure it does, but nothing could be more painful than watching the only person I have in the world fight for her life every single day. Nothing could be more torturous than wondering each time she closes her eyes if it will be the last."

255

He shook his head. "You say that now, but what happens when you realize that an eternity of damnation *is* worse? What if you realize what a foolish mistake you made? What if you regret your decision and wish that you could go back and do things over again?"

"I won't."

"I did not think so either, but I found I was wrong. I wanted only vengeance during those last days. I had failed Felice and so I needed to make it up to her by finding her murderer. By killing him. A life for a life. That's what I thought." He shook his head. "But there was no satisfaction in my actions. Just punishment. I don't want you to make the same mistake. I don't want you to give your all for such a foolish notion and then spend an eternity regretting it."

"I'll never regret my actions, and I'll certainly never regret loving Kara so strongly." She stepped toward him. "You didn't sacrifice for love, Cain," she told him, voicing her thoughts for the first time. "You killed that man out of fear. Because you feared losing the only person who'd ever loved you. You feared being alone and so you reacted based on that fear."

He flinched as if hit and she knew she'd struck a nerve. "I wasn't afraid," he said, but she knew the words were merely denial. She could see the truth in his gaze, feel it in her own heartbeat.

She felt him, just as he must feel her.

"You were afraid. I know because I've felt the

same fear. I don't know what I would do without Kara. Without someone to love me. Faced with the prospect, I was willing to do anything to avoid it coming to fruition. Even sell my soul." She took another step, her gaze steady with his. "It isn't your soul you regret losing, but the taking of another man's life. It's guilt, you feel. Not regret."

"He deserved to die. He killed the only person who'd ever loved me."

"But you didn't love her." Her words brought his head up. His gaze locked with hers and deep in the sea green depths she saw the truth. "You hunted down her killer out of duty. You killed him out of duty. Because you felt you owed her. She saved your life that day when she found you dying. She gave you a new chance at life. You loved her for that, but you didn't really love her. Not like she loved you."

Silence stretched between them disrupted only by the whir of the air conditioner blowing icy relief into the room. But it did little to ease the passion raging inside her. Or the compassion. For she felt both where Cain was concerned.

"I should have loved her," he finally said. "She deserved that from me."

"We can't choose who we love and who we don't love. It just happens." She turned away as the truth beat at her, demanding to be recognized.

257

The strange warmth she felt whenever he spoke of his past. The comfort he gave her with just a glance. The safety she felt in his arms. The bond she felt with him because he knew what it felt like to be lonely and unwanted as she had her entire childhood. The connection she felt because he'd learned later how it felt to be loved, just as she'd learned.

What about *to* love? Did he know what that felt like, as well? Did he know it as surely as she did?

There was only one way to find out.

"I didn't expect to fall in love with you," she blurted, the words forming on her lips before she could stop them. Not that she would have. The pressure in her chest was still there, a reminder of what she'd done and what she would eventually face.

Her own time was now limited.

Precious.

She didn't intend to waste a moment.

"I shouldn't even think such a thing," she went on. "It's totally crazy." She turned and her gaze locked with his. "But I can't help myself. I don't just think it. I feel it. I feel you." She touched her chest, her palm resting over her heart. "Right here."

Pleasure flashed in his gaze before it faded into a despair so profound it reached out and twisted at her rapidly beating heart. For she knew that Cain had known so little love in his life. He'd had parents who would have loved him, but they'd died. He'd been shunned by society until Felice. She'd turned his life around and given him love and he'd taken it like a starving man devouring crusts of bread. Even then, he'd never felt the emotion deep down in his bones. It was a wondrous feeling to be loved. But even more joyous, was to actually love in return. To feel the emotion for someone else who shared your feeling.

There was nothing like it.

Sophie knew that firsthand.

She'd grown up without loving parents, as well, though that had been by choice rather than death. She'd longed for the emotion herself until Gwen and Ed and Kara. They'd given her the love of family that she'd longed for her entire life. A feeling she'd reciprocated.

For the first time, the emotion hadn't been merely one-sided and so she'd been fulfilled. At least as far as family went.

She'd never known the feeling with a man.

Likewise, Cain had never known love with a woman.

As sad as the realization made her, she felt happy, as well. Hopeful. That maybe he felt such an emotion for her.

Temporary.

They had no future. She knew that. Cain's forever was already mapped out for him, and Sophie had sacrificed hers. Already, she felt herself slipping away. They had only this moment.

"Perhaps I don't desire you."

"You desire all women. You said so yourself, yet you held back from me. Why?"

"You complicate things."

"Why?"

He shook his head. " 'Tis crazy."

"I love you."

" 'Tis lust, not love that you feel for me, sweet Sophie."

"It's both." She stepped forward then, completely closing the distance between them. With the wall at his back, there was no place for him to go and Sophie took full advantage. She touched her lips to his.

Every muscle in his body went rigid and she half expected him to push her away. She felt the push-pull of feelings inside him. He wanted to kiss her, yet he didn't.

"Stop," he finally gasped, pushing her away from him. "I cannot do this. I will not."

"Why?"

"Because." He shook his head, as if still battling with something. Or someone. "I won't let you throw it all away."

"I've already given up my soul. It's over, Cain. We have only right now. Only this moment to claim whatever happiness we can with one another."

He shook his head and slid his hands down to twine his fingers around hers. His body started to shake as he slid his hands around until her palms met his.

The trembling grew stronger, his muscles jumping, his body quaking as an unseen force gripped him. He stared at her, into her, but he didn't see her. He saw something else that frightened him.

He saw her future.

Hell and damnation.

The reality of what awaited her now that the discovery had been made, the bargain complete.

She felt a moment's fear for what she'd done, for what awaited her, and then it faded in a fierce rush of compassion for the man who held her hands so tightly, his eyes bright with tears.

Tears for her.

"Stop." She yanked free of his grip and placed her hands on his shoulders and tried to calm him. "Stop!"

He trembled a few more seconds before recognition finally lit his eyes and his gaze registered on her.

"I am sorry, Sophie. So sorry."

"You have nothing to be sorry for. This was my choice."

"But I can stop it."

For a moment, it struck her odd that he talked about the bargain in the present tense, as if it weren't already complete and Sophie hadn't lost her soul.

"You can't stop anything, Cain. It's over and done with. Forget the future, Cain. There is no future for us." She said the words matter-of-factly, but they brought a rush of tears to her eyes anyway.

Regret for what they would never have.

She forced the thought away and gathered her determination. "I can let that knowledge cripple me, or I can make enough memories right now to console me through whatever comes. Please." She touched his face when he tried to turn away. "I know what I've done and I know what I want to do. I don't want to think about tomorrow. I want to concentrate on right now. I want this time with you. I want you."

She pressed her lips to his. He resisted for one long moment, and then he seemed to come to some decision. His mouth opened and his tongue darted out to dance with hers in a long, delicious, hot kiss that took her breath away and left her wanting more.

"I want you," he said as he pulled away and stared down at her. "And I intend to have you."

Chapter Fourteen

His lips smothered hers and he thrust his tongue deep and the world fell away for several long, delicious seconds.

Sophie wasn't even aware of being lifted until she felt the mattress at her back. The bedsprings protested as Cain eased her down and followed and she realized he'd carried her into the bedroom.

The door was closed, blocking out the rest of the world, the walls a thick barrier to keep them from being disturbed. The moon pushed past the partially open drapes to give the room a surreal quality.

But this was real.

And the man pressing her down into the bed, covering her, surrounding her, was just as real.

Straddling her, his knees trapping her thighs, he leaned back to gaze down at her.

The ethereal light that pushed into the room haloed his broad, powerful form and made him seem more shadow than man.

All except for his eyes.

She saw them clearly, glowing green fire that burned her features and made her forget the heartbreaking past. The damnable future. Everything but now.

He was the unknown . . . a demon lover come to seduce and claim, a black silhouette fused by an undeniable force that drew her like a rebellious fourteen-year-old to a shiny tube of red lipstick.

She blinked. She had to be imagining him. She had to be dreaming again . . . just a very erotic fantasy.

But the hands that spread over her rib cage were more than figments of her very vivid imagination. They were strong and warm and determined as they unfastened the buttons of her blouse and slid the silk aside.

With a flick of his fingertip, he unfastened her bra clasp and bared both her breasts. Then his hands went to her waist. He undid her pants and pushed them down, his fingertips stroking bare flesh as he urged them down and pulled them free. Tossing them to the side, he turned his attention back to her panties. He shoved them down, until they collapsed around her ankles. With her toe, she slid them free of her feet and let them fall to the bed.

Her blouse disappeared completely as he urged her up and slid her arms free. Her bra followed until she lay completely open and exposed to him.

"I've wanted you like this for so long," he said, his voice thick and raw and unsteady. "Beneath me, open for me, wet for me . . . The memory of your dreams sustained me in purgatory during the long days, until the shadows fell and I could see you for myself. Smell you. Touch you. But I couldn't really do all that I wanted because so much stood between us." He leaned down and flicked his tongue at one nipple. "But there's nothing between us now." His breath fanned her sensitive flesh.

Her nipple responded, hardening and throbbing with a life all its own, begging for more than the one decadent lick and the rush of his breath.

More.

Lifting his arms, he peeled his T-shirt over his head and tossed it to the side. His hands went to his button and zipper and with one deft motion, the ends hung open. He didn't take his pants off. Not yet. As if he doubted his control should he shed his clothes completely.

"I tried to resist," he went on, his fingertips going to her abdomen. He traced lazy circles, touching, relishing as if he'd never felt anything

265

as soft. "To keep you from making an even bigger mistake that will haunt you for the rest of eternity, but I know that it's not my choice. It's yours and you've already made it. This is the inevitable for us, Sophie. It's what I'm meant to do. What you want me to do, and so now it must be done."

She searched for her voice, to beg him for answers to the questions swirling in her mind. Then he lowered his head and drew her nipple fully into the moist heat of his mouth, and her thoughts fled.

Sophie dug her fingers into the cotton sheets, falling victim to the warmth of his mouth.

He suckled her breast as if he were a hungry child, his teeth grazing the soft globes, nipping and biting the crested peaks until she cried out.

Not from pain, but pleasure. Pure, mind-blowing sensation as her breast swelled and throbbed with a need all its own.

Cain licked a path across her skin to coax the other breast in the same torturous manner.

A decadent heat spiraled through her and she moved her pelvis against the hard warmth of his hair-dusted chest. She wanted him, surrounding her, inside of her, consuming her, filling up the emptiness inside once and for all.

Sophie unclenched her fingers from the bed sheets to twine her arms around Cain's shoulders. She stroked down his arms, feeling the ripple of muscle, the soft silk of hair until her hands rested atop his.

That's when he pulled away.

"Cain?"

His eyes glowed in the darkness, like two emerald fires suspended in a pitch-black sky. A shiver worked its way up her spine when his deep, husky voice murmured, "Don't touch my hands. You can touch any part of my body, but not my hands."

"Don't be afraid of what you see in my future."

He shook his head. "This isn't about seeing. It's about feeling." He slipped his hands from beneath hers and touched her again. "The hunger gnawing in your belly." He swept his fingertips down, tracing slow circles across her abdomen. "The wetness between your thighs . . ." He went lower.

One rough fingertip traced the soft folds between her legs, pushing inside just a delicious fraction that made her quiver and gasp. "The heat deep, deep inside . . ." He pushed all the way in and she moaned, coming up off the bed as pure pleasure pierced her brain.

The feeling was consuming and exquisite and she couldn't so much as breathe for a long moment. He didn't move, just held himself deep inside as her body settled around him, clamping tighter, pulling him deeper.

"Do you understand?"

She nodded, her voice nonexistent in the face of such sensation. He'd touched her and tantalized her in her dreams, but it had never felt quite like this. So bold and intense and delicious.

"Those were dreams. This is more."

"You can read my thoughts."

"Not from the outside." He moved his finger slightly. "But I am inside you and we are one. I can hear your thoughts as clearly as I can hear my own."

"And you can hear mine."

His deep voice registered in her head and she realized that he spoke the truth. They were connected at the moment. *One.*

Still, she wanted more. A complete possession.

"So do I, sweet Sophie. And we shall have it. Soon. Now just settle back and feel me. Feel the way I make you feel."

He pulled away from her then. Her thighs trembled and she barely fought the urge to grip him and pull him back. She would have, but he shook his head. He captured her wrists and urged them up over her head.

Obediently, she slid her hands beneath the pillow, the motion arching her breasts in silent invitation.

Cain smiled, his teeth a startling break in the black shadow of his face. Then the expression faded as he gazed down at her, his attention traveling from her face, down the column of her neck to her breasts and lower still.

His study was slow and thorough and stirring . . . So very stirring.

"I want you more than I've ever wanted any woman before . . . or after," he whispered, his voice low and fierce.

"And I want—"

He silenced her with his mouth, kissing her until she could barely breathe much less speak. Then he touched her, sliding his hands from her wrists to her shoulders. With a fierce possessiveness, he continued his trek over her collarbone, down the creamy fullness of her breasts, to her turgid nipples. A sharp breath caught in her throat as one fingertip traced her, pulling and plucking and making her moan.

"You're more beautiful than any woman. Softer. More responsive. Sweeter," he murmured before his head dipped and he drew her nipple deep, his teeth rasping against her sensitive flesh.

She cried out, her body arching into his mouth as he laved and sucked and licked. She writhed beneath him, clutching the pillow, silently begging for the release only he could give her.

He slid down her body, now slick from the fever that raged inside of her, and left a blazing path with the velvet tip of his tongue. With a gentle pressure, he parted her thighs. Almost reverently, he stroked the soft, slick folds between her legs.

She was wet and throbbing and he swore softly at the discovery. Tremors seized her body when she felt his warm breath blowing softly on her most sensitive area. Then his lips pressed against the inside of her thigh, nibbling a sweet, torturous path to the part of her that burned the hottest.

She gasped as his tongue parted her. He eased his hands under her buttocks, holding her to him, his shoulders urging her legs farther apart until she lay completely open and vulnerable. He nuzzled her for a long moment, drinking in her scent and prolonging the anticipation. And then with a heated curse, he devoured her, every thrust of his tongue, every caress of his lips, a raw act of possession that told her he'd never touched a woman or tasted a woman quite like her.

The truth fed her desire and she arched against him, eager to feel more, to get closer, to become one with him. To be undeniably and irrevocably *his*, once and for all.

One hot night.

The words whispered through her head and she embraced them, eager to ignore the tightening in her chest that reminded her of her completed bargain and the fact that she'd lost her soul to the Devil and he would undoubtedly come to claim it.

Soon.

Before she could dwell on the thought, the sensation inside her built and she exploded. Waves of heat washed over her until she burned so fiercely, she felt certain she would disintegrate. But Cain was there, holding her, anchoring her until the heat subsided.

Only when she had calmed to a slight shudder, did he pull away from her. Moments later, he glided his body over hers and gathered her in his powerful arms.

Skin met skin as he settled over her, blocking out everything except the sight and sound and smell of him. His eyes glittered with jade fire. Rasping breaths parted his sensual lips. The steamy scent of sex, heat and aroused male filled the air. Muscle corded his body, flexing and bunching with every movement.

"I . . ." she started, suddenly eager to tell him what she was feeling.

The wonder.

The heat.

The raw emotion.

He silenced her with a kiss and she sampled her own essence. The taste—like ripe fruit both bitter and sweet at the same time—sent a spurt of hungry desire through her. She met his kiss with an erotic fervor that wrung a low, deep moan from his throat.

Strong hands roamed over her body, arousing every nerve, making her want and crave him in a way more intense that anything she'd ever felt before.

Even in her dreams.

Especially in her dreams, for they had been nothing more than her very vivid imagination.

This was real.

Cain was real.

Right here and now, at this moment, he was every bit a man. *The* man.

The only man for her.

The thought rooted despite her best efforts to push it aside. He wasn't a man, she knew that and yet she didn't believe it. He felt too real. Too warm.

But it wasn't so much the way he felt to her, but the way he felt *for* her . . .

More than just desire. Much more. There was no mistaking the reverence in his touch, the possessive heat that glowed in his gaze and it was no wonder she'd fallen in love with him.

She wanted to touch him so badly at that moment, and she did. Her hands slid around his neck and he went stock still.

"No—" he started, but she silenced him with her fingertips.

"Yes. I need to touch you, Cain. To feel you the way that you're feeling me."

She saw the turmoil in his gaze, felt it in the tense set of his muscles. But then she traced a fingertip along his cheek and cupped his face.

He closed his eyes and nuzzled into her touch, as if relishing her warmth.

"I won't touch your hands," she added, "I promise. But I need to touch you. Please."

As if he couldn't resist the plea any more than he could her caress, he nodded.

Her hand slid down, fingertips tracing the column of his throat as she wrapped her arms around him and threaded her fingers through the soft silk of his long blond hair.

Every notion she'd ever had about love and happily ever after rushed through her mind at that moment and the truth crystallized in her mind.

She'd given herself to Cain not out of lust, because he was safe and temporary, but because he was the man she loved. She didn't want him because he couldn't give her a morning after. She loved him in spite of it.

And he loved her.

While he didn't say the words, she felt them in his touch as he began a thorough exploration of her body, his hands caressing pleasure points she never knew existed.

She stroked the small of his back, rubbed against him, both thrilled and frightened by his pulsing length, which pressed into her stomach. He was rock hard and deliciously warm, and Sophie found herself wanting to feel his length inside of her.

"Please, Cain," she breathed. "I need you inside me so bad. I've never wanted anything so much."

"Please, what?" He kissed and stroked and nuzzled while waiting for her answer. "What exactly do you want me to give you?"

"Pleasure," she breathed.

He growled, a low barbaric sound that spooked as much as it delighted. Still, she refused to be frightened.

But when she felt the tip of his arousal probe the moist entrance to her womanhood, the small niggling of fear grew more insistent. She wanted to run, yet she also wanted to stay.

"And what will you give me in return?" he murmured, his tongue licking the shell of her ear. He eased just a fraction inside her and she whimpered.

"Please, I need you." She stared into his eyes, seeing her own desire in his gaze. "I need you more than I've ever needed anyone." She felt the moisture in her eyes and she tried to blink it back, but it was no use.

A tear slid free, for the admission came from more than a demand for physical gratification. She'd let Cain closer to her than she'd ever let any man. He knew her hopes and dreams. He knew of her love for Kara, of her promise to Gwen.

He knew her emotionally and now she wanted the physical intimacy, as well. She wanted everything from him.

And in return, she would give everything.

"Whatever you want—" but he stopped her with a swift thrust of his hips as he impaled her on his rigid length. All thought faded into a rush of pleasure.

"No more talk," he growled, his expression fierce as if he'd come to some silent conclusion. "Just feel me," he murmured, his voice raw and husky. "Feel us."

And she did.

Her fingers loosened from the sheets and she skimmed her hands over the sinewy flesh of his back. He flexed his buttocks and began to move steadily, penetrating deeply. His hands played over her body, touching and caressing, building the pressure inside her. He sucked and licked her nipples until she was panting and moaning and clinging to him.

The pressure built inside her, like a newly ignited spark being fanned into a full-blown flame. The heat spread, the fire growing, raging higher as Cain moved inside her. The pressure grew until it became unbearable and she went over the top.

The darkness seemed to come alive around them then, the shadows stirring and dancing. Thunder rumbled in the distance and despite her state of arousal, she remembered what Beth had said about the weather.

The sky is clear. Not a thunder cloud in sight.

As if to defy her thoughts, a bolt of lightning

cracked open the sky outside the window and she glimpsed Cain poised above her, his arms braced on either side, muscles bulging, skin glistening with perspiration. He held his eyes clamped shut, his lips parted, his forehead furrowed.

He shook with the violence of his release and she bucked against him, drawing him fully inside, relishing the spurt of warmth.

For the first time in her life, as Sophie stared up at the man she loved above all others, she felt complete.

Enough!

The word shattered the stillness surrounding them and the tightness in her chest intensified. The air seemed to come alive around them, moving and whispering. Another bolt of lightning cracked open the sky and shattered the window.

Glass flew as a fierce wind whipped into the room.

A tornado.

That's what Sophie thought, what it felt like as the wind kicked up their surroundings, ripping the curtains from the walls and lifting furniture.

And then it came.

Like a giant black fist that reached inside and gripped Cain.

The darkness pulled at him, ripping them apart.

"No!" Sophie scrambled to her feet and reached for him, but it was too late. The pitch black tightened its grip, closing around him and pulling him into the nothingness.

She caught a glimpse of his face before the darkness completely consumed him. His eyes flashed with fear and his face twisted in pain and then he was gone, swallowed up by the dark beast itself.

The wind settled and the thunder ceased and the only sound that remained was the frantic beat of her heart.

Sophie climbed to her feet, her legs trembling as she walked to the window and stared at the quiet street below.

Quiet.

As if nothing had happened.

As if her heart hadn't just been ripped out of her chest.

"No," she breathed, fighting for her next breath. Fighting against the truth.

Gone.

He was gone and it was over and now there would be hell to pay. Literally.

She felt it in the tightness of her chest. Oxygen burned her lungs as her nostrils flared and she tried to breathe. The effort was useless, just as she was useless.

She couldn't save Cain from whatever had taken him anymore than she could save herself.

Ah, but she'd saved Kara.

She held the knowledge close as she struggled to get control of her pounding heart. If only she could breathe. But the air hurt. It smelled. A burning scent that made her eyes water and her legs tremble.

She fought to grab the sheet and wrap it around her.

Her legs. She had to make her legs work, to walk down the hall and check on Kara.

She couldn't seem to lift her feet.

"This can't be happening," she murmured, trying to understand why her body didn't want to cooperate.

Breathe, her brain instructed.

She tried, just as she tried to walk, to see past the few feet in front of her. But the room had started to move again, alive with a force all its own, or so it seemed.

Until she heard the voice and realized that what was happening to her wasn't the same as what had happened to Cain.

Her threat was very real, and he was wearing black leather gloves.

"No," she murmured, seeing the shape move in the corner and advance toward her. She stumbled backwards. "You can't do this."

"But I can." The hands reached for her.

Sophie caught a fleeting glimpse of a gloved hand as it rushed toward her.

Pain exploded in her skull and her legs gave out. She sank to the floor.

278

Breathe, her brain kept screaming, but her body didn't want to cooperate. Her heartbeat slowed and her worry dissolved and the pain in her head dulled to an ache.

Then she felt nothing.

Chapter Fifteen

He watched her, only now it wasn't via video surveillance tape. This was the real thing.

Sophie Alexander in the flesh.

He pushed up from the chair where he'd been sitting for the past hour, watching and waiting for her to regain consciousness, and crossed the room to her.

She was still out thanks to the chemical-soaked rag he'd held to her nose. That and the portable gas cylinder he'd turned on inside the bedroom while she'd been doing the nasty with some unexpected someone.

Out of all the surveillance he'd had done on her, complete with wire taps and bugs, he'd never heard mention of a boyfriend or lover.

Until tonight.

He hadn't actually seen the man. He'd merely turned the knob and pushed the cylinder just inside the doorway, just as he'd done down the hall in Kara's room. Then he'd settled back to wait while the gas took effect.

The child would be out for hours, for she was much smaller than her godmother with less resistance to the fumes. And so he'd had to use an additional measure to make sure that Sophie lost consciousness long enough for him to get the situation under control. He'd approached her room with the ether-soaked rag and the gas cylinder, armed with two means to his end.

He'd heard the ruckus inside the room just when he'd been about to turn the knob. At first, he'd been surprised to hear more than one voice. While he'd had her under surveillance, not once had the reports or video tapes eluded to a significant other.

Obviously, she had one, at least for the night. He'd tried to push the door open anyway, not in the least put off by the presence of someone else. He was too intent on his goal to let another person get in his way. He would simply deal with the situation the same way he intended to deal with Sophie.

But first, the gas cylinder . . .

He'd tried to push open the door and set the cylinder inside, but something had stopped him. Only when the quiet settled in had he been able to open the door. He'd found a mess and right in the middle of it had stood Sophie Alexander.

Alone now and frightened.

He'd smiled then, for it was really perfect, after all.

He'd intended to do away with her with a well-placed bullet and a suicide note to explain it away, but the after-hours liason and the shattered window would prove an even more convincing means of death.

She'd had sex, they'd argued and her lover had left. She'd thrown herself out the window, or better yet, been pushed by said lover who'd then fled the scene.

An affair gone awry.

He smiled as he surveyed her. She lay on her back on the bed she'd shared with her lover such a short time ago. The sheets were a tangled mass on the floor, the bare mattress cushioning her back. Glass littered the floor. The curtains lay in a shredded mess. He'd looked for some sign of the man, but had found nothing. His guess had been that the guy had gone out the window. He hadn't jumped for there was no mess below.

No police or ambulance.

Perhaps they'd had a fight and Mr. Significant Other had left.

That's the conclusion he'd drawn after he'd surveyed the scene.

He sniffed and wiped at his runny nose, careful to fold the napkin he'd brought and stuff it back into his pocket. He would leave no evidence behind. Not a trace of his visit. No footprints thanks to the socks he now wore—his shoes at the door. No fingerprints thanks to the leather gloves. The lab had been left just as neat, as if an unseen force had slipped a hand in and retrieved the notes and experiment findings. Not a file had been disturbed, everything as neat and orderly as it had been found. It would be as if the formula never existed.

He smiled. Things were progressing nicely. The smell had all but disappeared by now as it would completely before her body was discovered. He knew that firsthand because he'd carefully planned every aspect of this game.

After all, he played to win.

He nudged her and she stirred, her sigh muffled by the rag tied around her mouth. Her legs were tied along with her wrists. A slipknot he'd learned in a sailboating class several summer's ago when he'd actually had the time for vacations.

Before his work had overwhelmed him and he'd become centered in life.

You have to have goals, son. You have to see what you want and go after it, letting nothing stand in your way. Your life is what you make of it. You control your destiny and all in its path. Don't ever let anyone tell you differently.

That's what his father had always told him.

When he'd had the time to actually speak. He'd been centered around his career, as well, leaving the rearing of his only son to a string of well-paid nannies.

He'd felt neglected sometimes, wishing that his father could have been at this class event or that T-ball game. When he'd grown up, however, he'd understood. A man had to have priorities. To go after what he wanted with ruthless intent. To be the best at all cost, even at the sacrifice of his self and his family.

He didn't have a family now. He'd never married, never fathered any children of his own. His father was long gone, dead from a stress-induced heart attack because he'd let all of his sound advice fall by the wayside and fallen victim to his job. He'd let the job take control of him, rather than the other way around. A big mistake.

One his son had no intention of repeating.

He was the master of his universe, guiding his life the way he wanted it to go. *Up*. He wanted to go all the way to the top, to be *the* best, and Sophie Alexander was a stepping stone to that position.

A shame, really. She was a beautiful woman. Smart. Dedicated. He admired her tenacity. She'd stuck with her ridiculous aspirations despite his best efforts to dissuade her. She'd been stubborn and she'd kept on, and lo and behold, she'd actually discovered something.

He still couldn't believe the computer notes he now had in his possession. Thanks to the top-notch private investigator who'd been doing surveillance on her. He'd recorded everything in her lab via a wireless bug, and had slipped into the lab the minute she'd left to retrieve the notes.

An easy task for a veteran who'd been on both sides of the law. The investigator had been able to slip easily by the security team recently hired by her company. As for the security codes . . . *like taking candy from a baby*, or so his man had told him.

Of course, the job had cost more than anticipated. He'd given the investigator top dollar, as well as a bullet from the gun he now held. After all, he couldn't leave any loose ends untied and a private detective would have linked him to Sophie.

He wasn't a big fan of murder, but a man had to do what a man had to do with his reputation and career riding on the line. The formula was, afterall, the discovery of a lifetime.

His discovery, or it soon would be once Sophie was completely out of the picture.

He stroked her dark, lustrous hair before heading back to the small pack that sat in the far corner. Retrieving his gun, he settled down in his chair and checked the silencer.

The ABC's of firearms was another class he'd taken way back when. He didn't intend to use the weapon now for anything more than a persuasive device. But he had the silencer on just in case another curve ball came his way once Sophie Alexander opened her eyes.

"Wake up, Sophie. It's time to wake up."

The familiar voice came from far away, pushing its way into Sophie's conscience. She knew the voice and yet something didn't fit.

The voice didn't belong here.

"Wake up."

She tried, but her body ached and her eyelids felt too heavy for her to do more than blink at first. Her head pounded and the throbbing in her temples kept time with the steady tick of a clock somewhere in the room.

Her room. She knew it. She felt the familiar softness of her bed, but she wasn't nestled into it for a good night's sleep. Her wrists hurt and the sides of her mouth felt raw and swollen and her feet . . . She couldn't seem to do more than move her toes.

She blinked again, forcing her eyes open against the blinding light trained on her. A flashlight she realized when the light shifted and she caught a glimpse of the shadow behind it.

"It's about time you came to."

"I . . ." She struggled to speak, but the word was barely audible thanks to the rag tied at the back of her head. Her tongue felt heavy, her mouth dry as cotton, the corners of her lips raw and tender.

She concentrated all of her efforts on focusing her eyesight. The flashlight beam snaked across the room before dying a quick death as the shadow flicked it off. She blinked several times, letting her watery eyes adjust to the dimness. Outside her bedroom window, the moonlight glowed, pushing into the room and lighting its interior.

Shards of glass caught the light and twinkled back at her, and reality rushed through her. For the next few heartbeats, she relived the past few hours since making her discovery. She remembered her declaration to Cain and their sweet lovemaking, and the hell that followed. The thunder and the lightning and the darkness and Cain being swallowed up by some unseen force.

Tears burned her eyes and slid silently down her cheeks and the light flicked on again. She forced her eyes shut against the blinding ray of a flashlight.

"You are awake. Good."

The light flicked off again and Sophie opened her eyes. A few blinks and she focused on the shadow standing over her. She couldn't make out his face until he leaned back and turned, and moonlight spilled over his familiar features.

"It's about time you came to. I'm on a schedule, you know," Dr. Chris Stevens told her. In stark contrast to his usual white lab coat, he wore a black shirt and matching pants, like the dark alter ego of the good doctor she saw every time she and Kara visited the hospital. "I've got rounds first thing in the morning."

Questions rushed through her mind, none of which came out as more than unintelligible garble.

"What? Surprised to see me?" He smiled, his teeth a stark-white break in the shadows. "I can see why you might be. I heard all about the alleged espionage theory. I must say, it was a little far-fetched, but then that boss of yours has a hard-on for her ex so I can see why she would want to point the finger at him. Honestly, the man merely got lucky last year when he duped you guys. Thanks to members of your marketing team, of course. Those people are always bragging and tooting their horns before it's time. That's how he made the discovery. Sheer luck.

"He isn't even close to anything as groundbreaking as *Forever Young*. As for me—" He indicated the bag that sat in the far corner and she knew without even seeing the contents, that he held her future in the canvas sack. "I am very close." He pinned her with a frown. "Despite your lack of cooperation. You hadn't been giving me much during our phone calls, so I had to see for myself if you were really on to something. I must say, I was pleasantly surprised."

She tried to process everything he was saying, but her head hurt too much for her to do more than blink. And pray.

As if anyone would hear her. She'd sold her soul, and then she'd lost her heart. There was no one to hear her except Kara—

Her thoughts stumbled to a halt and her eyes widened. She tried to speak, but only a sharp cry came out.

Where was Kara? Was she all right? Had Dr. Stevens gotten to her already or would she come after Sophie?

She shook her head, fighting against the truth as she tried to get a grip on the fear holding her paralyzed.

Think. Calm down and think.

She tried to slow the pounding of her heart and tune in to her surroundings.

". . . love to untie you," Dr. Stevens was saying, "but I can't risk any noise. It's a wonder you and that gymnastics expert you had in here earlier didn't wake the entire building with all your ruckus. You surely would have woken up poor Kara if I hadn't gotten to her first."

No. Even as denial raged in her head, she knew he spoke the truth. He'd dealt with Kara. Silenced her.

No . . . !

Tears blinded her and despair welled inside. She tried to move, fighting against her ties. She had to get loose. To see for herself—

The thought ground to a halt as she caught a streak of white in the corner of her eye. Her gaze shifted past Dr. Stevens to the open doorway and she saw a touch of white against the doorframe.

The edge of a nightgown.

"Damn, but you two made some noise." He shook his head, drawing her attention again as he motioned to her. That's when she noted the gun in his hand. Fear, fresh and fierce, erupted inside her, but she refused to be crippled. Kara stood just behind him and Sophie had to stay calm. To figure a way out.

"But it's been as quiet as a medical seminar after the last scheduled speaker," Dr. Stevens went on. "Those doctors . . . Never ones to sit around asking questions. They think they know all the answers themselves."

Sophie shifted her gaze back to the doorway. Kara peered around the edge and for a split-second, their gazes locked.

Hide.

Sophie mouthed the word, but she wasn't sure Kara would understand with the rag hindering her communication.

She tried again. *Hide.* This time the little girl nodded. She disappeared and Sophie was left to face Dr. Stevens on her own.

"You look pale, Sophie. Like you've seen a ghost."

No.

Not yet.

Not ever if Kara did as she was told and hid someplace that Chris Stevens couldn't find her.

"Why, I bet you're just a little confused by all of this. I'm sure you must have a million questions, don't you, Sophie? You do. I can see it in your eyes and though I'm on a schedule, I'll enlighten you just a little. After all the work you've done, it's the least I can do. In fact, that's what it's all about—the work. My work once you're dead and unable to refute the announcement of my major discovery."

"But—" she started. The rag moved and cut into her mouth and she winced.

"You see, this is my field of expertise. I'm the known specialist in this area. I've spent my entire life working on therapies to treat cancer patients. I've spent hour after hour doing research and I've come up with nothing. The new laser therapy is revolutionary, but it pales in comparison to what *Forever Young* can do. It pales, and I can't have you showing me up, can I? I know, I know. You were going to give the formula to me for further development, but it still wouldn't be mine. Your name would go in the text books as the genius behind it, not mine." He shook his head. "I can't have that and so you have to die."

"No—" She tried again, but the rag prevented anything more than what sounded like a moan from coming out.

"I know, I know. You'll give me full credit." He shook his head. "Not good enough, I'm afraid. There would always be the chance that you could refute your earlier words and tell people the truth. No, this is the best way. The only way."

And he stepped toward her.

Kara crawled deep into the closet, pulling clothes and stuffed animals over her. She crouched into a ball and closed her eyes, praying the way she always did when the fear overcame her or when she felt sick to her stomach or when she would rather keep her eyes closed than face another day filled with so much pain.

"Please," she whispered.

As always, a warmth surrounded her, embracing her and cradling her close the way her Aunt Sophie did whenever Kara had a bad dream and crawled into her bed.

This warmth was just as good as Aunt Sophie's arms. In fact, with her eyes closed, she could actually feel arms holding her close and hear a heart pounding in her ear.

So slow and steady and reassuring.

It's going to be all right, little one. Very soon, everything is going to be all right.

The sweet voice whispered in her ear and she knew it was her guardian angel. She wanted to open her eyes, to see the familiar face that had stared down at her night after night, after she'd said her prayers and crawled into bed.

She would feel the dip in her mattress, followed by the warmth and she would open her eyes to see the angel who was hers and hers alone.

Her guardian angel, just as the man she'd seen the other night was Sophie's guardian angel.

"Please let him be with her now," she whispered the prayer, knowing deep in her heart that someone listened.

Someone who could help them out of the terrible trouble that waited just on the other side of the closet door.

Do not worry, child. It shall be done.

She felt the hands then, so soft and soothing and comforting. Stroking her forehead, her cheeks, her hair.

Kara smiled and nuzzled the stuffed Raggedy Ann in her arms. Warmth cloaked her, soothed her, and she settled down to wait.

"You failed me." The familiar voice cut through the thick darkness that held Cain captive.

He tried to open his eyes, but the onslaught of light forced them shut again. Still, he felt the presence, cold and intense, like a wall of ice that surrounded him.

But it wasn't ice he saw when he managed to finally open his eyes. It was fire. Flames. A circle of orange that surrounded and caged him.

Just beyond the circle stood the Evil One looking every bit as cold and frightening and evil as his name in a flame-red gown that matched the brightness of his eyes.

The fire flared and forced Cain's eyes closed again.

"You were supposed to get her to give you the formula during your seduction. She was supposed to say the words," he growled, his voice thundering in the dark chamber where Cain now found himself imprisoned.

Cold stone seeped up through his feet and met his back. He was back in the castle where he'd watched Felice's murder. Only this time, he was the one being held prisoner. Taunted and tortured.

"She *had* to say the words." The voice came closer and Cain felt the brush of a robe against his bare shoulder.

He flinched as a searing pain ripped through his body. Waves of heat slammed over him to stir his blood into a frenzy and pull him from the darkness where he'd been lingering. Waiting.

The wait was over.

"She didn't say the words," the Evil One reminded him. "You didn't make her say the words."

"You have her soul. It's enough."

"Enough? I say when it's enough and I want more. I want that formula. I deserve it. She

294

wouldn't have made that discovery without me."

"She wouldn't have made it without me. Not you. It was my sight that helped her."

"At my instruction." Chilling laughter erupted and fingers followed the path of the robe, stroked over his bare shoulder and sliced deep.

Cain clenched his teeth against the pain, clamping down on his bottom lip until he tasted a salty sweetness.

"Oh my, you're bleeding." Another cackling laugh followed the mock concern. "And you shall bleed more because you defied me. I'm very disappointed in you, Cain. You were always my best incubus, always doing your duty like a good little boy, as if you enjoyed your servitude."

He hadn't enjoyed it as much as he'd needed it. With every woman he'd convinced himself that he was paying for his past, when all he'd really been doing was running from it. The more he felt, the less he had to think.

To remember.

To regret.

Sophie had changed all of that.

She'd helped him face his past once and for all. He was through running from it.

"You haven't saved her, dear boy. I will have her formula before all is said and done. This is merely a small setback, one I already intend to correct. Don't you know that Sophie isn't the only one after the formula? There is another who will gladly hand it over to me when I make him a bargain he can't refuse. Why, he'll be even easier to convince than she will. But, of course, I won't let this little act of defiance go unpunished. She'll have to pay for causing me to change my plans. And so will you."

"Leave her alone."

"I'll never leave her alone. You should know that now. Her soul is mine, as is yours." White heat sliced into his chest in a circular pattern a split second before he felt the fingers tighten around his heart. "Yes, Sophie is mine now."

Sophie.

Her name came like a rush of frigid wind, numbing him to the pain, fueling his strength.

He opened his eyes.

"If you hurt her, I'll kill you."

"Really? That, I must say, would be a miracle and I stopped believing in those centuries ago. Don't worry, dear boy, she'll be fine. I've always wanted to beef up my succubus regime. She'll make a nice addition. I'm sure many a man will fall victim to her seduction. Why, she'll probably give you a run for your money. And judging by last night, I'm sure she'll enjoy every moment. She's quite the little whore."

In a fierce rage, Cain fought against the manacles binding his wrists, pulling and twisting, fighting with everything he had.

"Go ahead," the Evil One taunted, "Fight with everything you have. Wear yourself down. You will never get free for this is your punishment now. Imprisonment here in the darkness with only your thoughts to keep you company. Think about her, Cain. Think about what you've done to her. You damned her for me. You spoiled her just as I am spoiling you."

A white hot pain wrenched through Cain's chest and he drew a breath through his teeth as the Evil One's claws sunk deep, cutting and twisting. Waves of heat jolted through him as his blood spilled on the stone floor of the dungeon where he hung suspended from the stone wall. He smelled the pungent odor of life, death and the afterlife—the place where time suspended itself, the pain gripping and excruciating.

Through glazed eyes, Cain watched as the Evil One pulled back only to come at him again. His nails dripped red. The Evil One laughed, the sound a muffled intrusion in Cain's mind that joined with the thunder of his heartbeat.

His *heart*.

He still had one. While the devil had stolen his soul, he hadn't taken Cain's heart, the source of his emotion, the fountain of his love.

Nothing could take that away from him. It was his to horde, just as it was his to give.

"Suffer," the Evil One told him, following the words with another sharp slash of his talons. "I have a youth formula to get my hands on. I'll give Sophie your best and tell her not to worry. You used her and now it's my turn."

"I didn't," he gasped through clenched teeth. The flames died and the Evil One's laughter faded and Cain gathered his strength in one last attempt. "I didn't use her. I loved her," he whispered. *"I love her!"*

And then the blackness closed in once again.

Cain was lost in his memories. That's what it had to be for he felt Sophie's soft hands near his, her fingertips grazing his bare flesh. He smelled the soft, sweet scent of her. He inhaled, drinking in the fragrance.

Something wasn't right. He forced his eyes open, expecting to see nothing but the usual oblivion. Instead, he caught a fleeting glimpse of long blond hair and piercing blue eyes.

"What . . . ?" he started, but the crackling sound of chains moving thundered through his head, temporarily killing his train of thought.

"Hush now and let me finish." Metal scraped and clicked and the pressure on his wrists fell away. The restraints on his ankles soon followed.

"I don't understand."

"Don't spend your time worrying over it. I shouldn't be here and neither should you. Not anymore." She pinned him with her deep blue gaze.

A gaze that sent a burst of warmth through him and eased the pain beating at his temples.

"Go to her," she told him. "Go to her because you love her. Because now you know what love is and you have a chance to prove it this time. You are free."

"But the Evil One—"

"I will deal with him when the time comes. *Go*."

Cain didn't need anymore encouragement. He stepped toward the swirling darkness.

"Come on," Chris said as he reached for Sophie. "Don't make this more difficult."

She struggled away from him, pushing and pulling and fighting for her life. But her efforts proved useless. He gripped her tied hands and hauled her toward the window.

"It's a long way down, but then your lover didn't consider that when he pushed you. He was merely consumed by his anger because you two had a fight. You were disappointed in his performance or, perhaps, overjoyed. You wanted a commitment, but he didn't and so things got ugly."

"Ah, but he does want a commitment." The familiar voice brought Sophie's head around and she glimpsed Cain behind her. "He wants so much more than one night." His gaze met hers. "I want you. Now and forever."

Relief welled inside her, followed by a rush

of fear when Dr. Stevens thrust her away and trained his gun on Cain.

"Ah, the angry lover comes back. All the better. We'll have a nasty push, followed by a suicide because one of you couldn't bear the thought of losing the other."

"You're right about part of that."

"The nasty push or the suicide?"

"The part about not bearing the thought of losing the other. I won't lose Sophie."

"Then you'll follow her to hell." He pushed Sophie over the edge and she closed her eyes as the wind hit her face and gravity pulled her over. She clutched at the window ledge, holding on for dear life as her legs dangled and her body weighed her down.

Inside, chaos erupted.

She heard Cain's shout, followed by a scuffle. Gunfire erupted, the silencer making the noise little more than a high-pitched *ping, ping* that echoed in her head as she held on to life.

"Hold on." The voice followed her, but it wasn't Cain's. She knew that and the knowledge forced her eyes closed. Her fingers clutched and re-clutched and she knew what waited for her.

She let go.

But hands grabbed for her, hauling her back over until she collapsed inside. Her gaze zeroed in on the man who'd pulled her in.

The doctor staggered backwards and collapsed from the chest wound oozing blood all over his shirt. Her gaze darted around the room, but she saw no one else.

Cain was gone.

She slumped against the wall as despair gripped her and the room seemed to swim. He couldn't be gone, yet there was no denying what had just happened. The doctor had saved her and now he was dying. And Cain was gone.

"Don't jump to conclusions. Have a little faith." The voice brought Sophie's head up and she saw Angela standing in the doorway.

It was Angela, but there was something different about her. The light . . .

A halo of light shown down around her, embracing her.

"What?" She caught Sophie's gaze. "Don't tell me you've never seen *Touched by an Angel?*"

"You're an *angel*?"

"Don't sound so shocked. I know I put on a good act as Angela, but I didn't think she seemed that unredeemable."

"She was just so hard. Too hard for an angel."

"Actually, I'm a guardian angel." She stepped aside and motioned behind her. Kara stepped forward, a Raggedy Ann clutched in her hands. Her huge eyes drank in the chaos of the bedroom before coming to rest on Sophie.

She smiled and slipped her hand into Angela's.

"I knew it," she told Sophie.

"Knew what?"

"She's been praying. Something you should have stuck with instead of going the other way. Then again, I can see why you did." She touched Kara's forehead, pushing back a strand of hair. There was a tenderness in the one motion that brought tears to Sophie's eyes and she knew the woman spoke the truth.

"She's a very special little girl," Angela went on. She turned to Sophie. "And you're special, too. You sacrificed for someone else and that touches the man upstairs, which is why I'm here."

"It's too late. I've already completed the bargain."

"It's never too late. Not for you, and not for Kara." She knelt at the child's feet. "You have a lot of faith for a little girl. I'd say that makes you deserving of a very special favor."

"Really?" Without waiting for an answer, she threw her arms around the woman's waist. "Thank you, Celeste."

"Celeste? I thought your name was Angela?"

"I was undercover." She smiled at Sophie. "You, too, have a lot of faith."

Sophie bowed her head, ashamed of herself for all that she'd done. For turning her back on the light and embracing the darkness. "I'm afraid I'm sorely lacking in that area."

"You have faith in love, Sophie." She leaned down and picked up the knapsack. "This discovery is the fruition of that faith." She eyed Sophie. "Give it to me."

"What do you mean?"

"Have a little faith and tell me that it's mine. That's the only way that I can protect it. If it belongs to me, I will be the owner and the Evil One will come after me. Not you. I am much more capable of dealing with him, believe me."

"I give my discovery to you," Sophie said.

Her words were followed by a loud grumbling. The sky cracked open with lightning, and thunder seemed to shake the entire building.

Sophie clutched the edge of the wall for support and Kara clung to the doorframe, but Celeste seemed unaffected.

Instead, she merely smiled and clutched the knapsack close. "He's just blowing off steam. He'll get over it. He's faced this before. I always win." Her gaze met Sophie's. "And you win, too, this time. You are also deserving of a very special favor. Of a very special future. You'll have one now, filled with light and love."

"There is no love." She stared at the empty spot where Cain had stood such a short time ago. Before the struggle and the gunshot. Her heart gave a painful thud and she closed her eyes against a blinding bout of tears.

No . . .

"Ah, but there is." Celeste's voice drew Sophie's eyes open in time to see the woman smile

303

at the slumped form of Dr. Chris Stevens. "All you have to do is believe."

And as Sophie followed her gaze and noted the rise and fall of his chest, a strange warmth filled her and she knew.

For she believed now, and joy filled her heart.

Epilogue

Sophie opened her eyes to the blinding sunlight and promptly clamped them back shut again. She snuggled into the warmth of the man next to her and lay there for several long moments just listening to the sounds around her.

Outside the large bay window that faced the east, the birds chirped out an early morning song. Inside, the sound of Saturday morning cartoons drifted from down the hallway, the *bleeps* and *What's up, Docs* mingled in with the sound of Kara's laughter.

The steady rise and fall of a hair-dusted chest pushed against her cheek. The soft, muted *thud, thud* of a heartbeat filled her ears.

She smiled and forced an eye open. Sure enough, the sight of that hair-dusted chest met her eyes and her moment's panic eased. No matter how many morning-afters she lived to enjoy with the man she loved, she would never quite believe that it was all real.

"It looks like someone had sweet dreams."

She glanced up at the deep sound of his voice and found herself staring at Dr. Chris Stevens. Yet at the same time, it wasn't him. In the six months that had passed since the incident, he'd changed. His hair had started to grow, plunging well past his collar now. The hot Texas sun had kissed his dark brown hair, making streaks of blond so reminiscent of the Viking he'd once been that she marvelled anyone could actually believe him to be the doctor.

But that was his identity. Only Sophie knew the truth. One that stared back at her in the form of a pair of fierce green eyes that filled her with a light and a love unlike anything she'd ever felt before.

"Actually, it's not my dreams that are sweet. It's my reality. Have I told you how much I love you today?"

"You're just buttering me up for all that firewood waiting to be chopped down by the creek. I can't believe it even gets cold enough in Texas to warrant gathering firewood."

"Not too often, but there are moments and I want to be ready to use that fireplace."

She wanted to make the most of every moment since the epiphany she'd experienced six months ago. The police had arrived that night and found nothing but a chaotic mess in her apartment and a wounded doctor who'd admitted to shooting himself during a suicide struggle.

His own, of course.

Dr. Stevens had been heartbroken that he couldn't find a cure for Kara. His entire staff knew how hard he worked for all his patients. And his desperation had driven him to confront Sophie about the new laser treatment chemotherapy program. She'd refused the treatment and he'd threatened to kill himself.

Sophie and Cain had collaborated on the story, with Kara and Angela Marks—Sophie's concerned co-worker—as witnesses. The incident had been written off. Cain had paid his visit to the hospital and taken over the role as Dr. Stevens.

His first order of business had been a huge donation which consisted not only of money, but Sophie's groundbreaking formula. He'd given Sophie the proper credit, handed over the formula to his research team and promptly resigned for health reasons.

At the same time, Beyond Beauty had launched its new product, *Forever Young*. Thanks to the pageant promotion, the product had taken off and catapulted the company back to the number one spot in its market. Carol had been so ecstatic that she'd offered Sophie a huge raise and promotion. Both of which she'd promptly turned down.

She needed a change of pace. A slower pace. Time to enjoy the new love she'd found with the man of her dreams.

She and Cain had wed five months ago, made the move to Gruene, Texas, and Gwen's old house, and now they were here with a very healthy and vibrant Kara.

Tears threatened her eyes and she blinked, still in awe of her good fortune.

Faith and love.

That's what had saved them all. Kara's faith and Sophie and Cain's love. Both had touched the Good One, who'd sent Celeste on his behalf.

She'd taken care of everything as promised, from Kara's clean bill of health to Cain's second chance as Chris Stevens.

It had been the doctor's time to go. When the bullet hit, his spirit had left his body and at Celeste's instruction, Cain had stepped inside.

Though possessing a living person for any length of time was impossible, this was different. This was a new body to house his spirit. A place for him to dwell and live out the rest of his days with the woman he loved. A second chance earned because of his own sacrifice. He'd defied the Evil One's specific instructions and let Sophie keep her precious formula, despite the torturous consequences.

The Evil One must surely have been angry,

but Celeste had dealt with his anger. She'd taken possession of the formula, passing it on to the team of experts as Dr. Stevens's faithful assistant, so as to keep it from the Evil One. With the formula no longer an issue, the Evil One had retreated back to hell to torment another lost and lonely soul.

Sophie and Cain were just people now, with nothing more at stake than their own lives, and so he would most likely leave them alone. Unless another weak moment struck and he thought he could gain their souls as he did others.

But their love would keep them strong and faithful. Celeste had assured them of that much.

He'd been freed from his bonds because of such love, because he'd felt deeply enough for Sophie to sacrifice his own future to save her from the Evil One. Likewise Sophie's sacrifice, her fierce love for a child, had earned her Kara's health.

The little girl was in permanent remission now. The doctors had called it a miraculous recovery, and Sophie knew how accurate their description was.

A miracle.

She'd been given a miracle for her sacrifice and for Kara's faith.

And on top of everything, she was expecting miracle number two.

"Is she kicking today?"

Sophie touched her growing stomach and her smiled widened. "What makes you so sure it's a she?"

"I just have a feeling. Besides, what man wouldn't want a house full of beautiful women to keep him company?"

"That's true." Her smile disappeared as she snuggled into his embrace.

"Did you call your parents?"

"If you're expecting them to be bowled over by the news, think again. They're not kid people, not even when it comes to their own child or grandchild. It's just the way they are."

A fact that no longer filled her with bitterness. She'd accepted her parents shortcomings and she loved them anyway. Even if they never reciprocated the emotion.

They *were* softening.

"Mother actually invited us for a visit. She said that she could take a few days off."

"That's something."

She smiled. "That's a major thing. Giving up a few days of work to meet her son-in-law? I was very impressed." And all the more intent on keeping the lines of communication open. No matter how hard she had to try.

She touched her lips to Cain's shoulder and relished the feel of warm, vibrant flesh. "If it's a girl, we're naming her Celeste," she told him.

"My thought exactly."

"I think she would like that."

Outside, the bright morning sun twinkled, sending rays of light dancing through the trees because Celeste liked it, very much. She liked it all, particularly the happy ending, very, *very* much.

Inside, Cain the Slayer drew the woman he loved above all others close to his heart and closed his eyes and gave thanks for his past, his present and his future with the woman in his arms.

He existed for her pleasure and hers alone. To love her and cherish her and give her back the sweet wonderful love she showered on him.

Now and always.